GOTHICK
or *NIGHTRIDE PRIORY*

Ian Lewis

a novel

Published by Waldorf Publishing
2140 Hall Johnson Road
#102-345
Grapevine, Texas 76051
www.WaldorfPublishing.com

Gothick

ISBN: 978-1-64921-471-3

Library of Congress Control Number:
2020940362

Copyright © 2020

All rights reserved. No part of this book may be reproduced or transmitted in any form or by any means whatsoever without express written permission from the author, except in the case of brief quotations embodied in critical articles and reviews. Please refer all pertinent questions to the publisher. All rights reserved. No part of this book may be reproduced or transmitted in any form or by any means, electronic or mechanical, including photocopying, recording, or by an information storage and retrieval system except by a reviewer who may quote brief passages in a review to be printed in a magazine or newspaper without permission in writing from the publisher.

Cover by Vova Kirichenko
Illustrations by Dariia Dziuba
Design by Baris Celik

Table of Contents

PRELUDE – BEFORE

THE CAVERN	2
THE HOUSE	10
THE LETTER	13

PART ONE – NOW

THE MESSAGE	19
HIGHWAYMAN	26
PISTOL	34
THE LONGEST NIGHT	38
THE DEVIL'S KIDNEYS	44
TWINS	48
COURAGE OF THE GENERAL	52
CAVENDISH SQUARE	59
AN EDUCATION	62
BLACKMAIL	65
REAP THE WHIRLWIND	68

PART TWO

LONDON PARTICULAR	72
ROOFTOPS	80
THE GENERAL RIDES	85
ACTORS	93
WATCHMEN	97
CONFUSE HER ENEMIES	101
JANE KNOWN AS SURI	105
THE GENERAL WALKS	112
TO FAVOUR CURRY	118
NIGHT ROOMS	129

BETRAYALS	134
SURROUNDED	142
DARKNESS AND DEPARTURE	145
THE UNWANTED SPY	151

PART THREE

LEAVING LONDON	157
THE VAULTS	165
NIGHT CREATURES	170
ANCIENT PLANS	176
THE HIGHWAY	181
DRY GRASS	186
THE COLD, COLD GROUND	192
THE ROLLING, ROLLING SEA	204
JUSTICE	214
THE GREY LADY	224
THE YEW TREE	230

PART FOUR

FUGITIVE	239
THE UNWISE ROAD	247
THE RIGHT SCHOOL	250
NEWGATE	260
SOLDIER, SOLDIER	265
TRAFFIC	277
COLONELS AND GENERALS	283
PAY THE FERRYMAN	286
VAGABONDS	296
HISTORICAL NOTE	302

PRELUDE – BEFORE

THE CAVERN

She has never been so terrified in her life. Or felt so good.

She stands hidden, just too far inside the cave for the moonbeams to reach. If she put out her sandaled foot, she could bathe it in pale gold – but then she would also be seen. She breathes in the damp smell of the cold stone – so refreshing after the heat of day that has been. "I'm standing between two worlds," she thinks, "the world out there, and in here the Underworld."

If she really listens, she can hear on one side the sounds of the night outside the cave, and on the other the sounds of water – drips echoing every few seconds, and, faintly, a stream running far in the depths of the cavern, down where they have never dared go, she and her friends from the village. But she enjoys knowing it's there. Their secret. She draws her sari tighter round her and shivers a little. Maybe one day they'll mount an expedition to explore that Underworld, she thinks. She giggles at the idea that she might Mount an Expedition.

She stands between worlds in more ways than one. She is fourteen years old. She and her father are English, and live (alone since her mother died) in a village in the Punjab, hundreds of miles from any of their countrymen.

In Europe, Napoleon's army is beginning its long, dying journey back from Moscow. In America, the new United States has launched an invasion of Canada. Neither news will reach India for some months yet. And there, somewhere in the north, Jane, known as Suri, stands in the shadow of a cave, admiring the moonlight on her toes and wondering how much longer she will have to wait.

Sandeep bet her that she would be too terrified to spend the night in the cave, because this is a place visited by the spirits of the dead – those who died in that great battle a thousand years ago. It's a place nobody dares come at night. But because she is *feringhi* – a foreigner – maybe she will be untouched by the curse of the place.

She fervently hopes that Sandeep is right and that the spirits will ignore her. She shivers again, but it's a delicious kind of excitement.

But where is Sandeep? The moonlight moves across the opening of the cave, and soon it no longer peers inside, and the surrounding trees hide the sky completely. It feels even darker because she is alone and thought her friend would be with her. She is beginning to feel lonely – and scared in ways that she no longer enjoys.

A night-bird cries. She should know what it is, but she is still too much a town-girl. She grew up in Amritsar – not a big city, but important – and she has never felt the need to learn the birds' names. She thinks of them much as she thought of the kites she and the boys flew from the rooftops in the evenings: beautiful flying things that don't need names.

But now there are other sounds. Men calling. Lights outside. Are they looking for her? Or do they hunt some other animal through the night?

Without thought, she shrinks back further into the darkness – the darkness becoming her friend again. In here she is safe.

She can see nothing, but feels the floor, dry and sandy. She goes further, because she is frightened of the men with their torches.

A sudden new sound makes her jump, and in leaping backward she bangs her head on the rock and falls to the ground.

She dreams. A half-dream, where she knows that she is asleep, and yet she feels the terror of what she sees, and hopes that it really is just a dream.

She seems to see her father lying bleeding on the road from Amritsar. He is reaching out towards her, and she sobs in fear and sorrow because she can't help him.

And she blinks as the sun warms her face. She is lying at the mouth of the cave, the warming day causing the scent to rise from the leaves by her head. Somehow, she has moved with the sunrise, towards the light. She sits up, wipes the sleep from her face, and rubs the sore patch on the back of her head.

As she leans back, her hand slides under the edge of the rock into a small hollow. She feels something hard – something not a stone. She scratches it free from the dirt and pulls it out into the daylight.

It's a jewel. A brooch. She shivers – a cold drop of dew down her spine. She knows she has never seen it before, and yet it seems familiar.

A shadow falls across her. A grunt of disapproval. The village Wise Woman stands looking down at her. With one hand she grips Sandeep tightly by the ear.

"What are you doing here, child? You and this skulking-in-the-bushes-boy," she gives another sharp tug on Sandeep's ear, smiling as he emits a thoroughly satisfying yelp. "You know it's forbidden," she continues.

Suri does know.

"I'm sorry," she begins.

"What is that in your hand?" the Wise Woman snaps. "Let me see."

But Suri doesn't want to let it go. "It was buried," she says. "But it's strange. As if it has always been mine, though I have never seen it before."

Sandeep is jumping up and down, even though the Wise Woman still holds him firmly by the ear. Either he's very excited, or he needs to find a private place behind a tree.

"Is this not the jewel your mother wears in her picture?" says Sandeep.

Of course it is. Suri gasps and closes her hand around it. Suddenly it's not just an interesting find, but something precious that she holds.

"How did you get it?" says Sandeep.

"It was just under here, under the rock."

"Let me see," grunts the Wise Woman. She glances at the brooch in Jane's hand and sniffs.

"Your mother must have dropped it

before she left."

Was that all? Jane expects something more ceremonial. She expects the Wise Woman to hold the brooch tightly in her hand, close her eyes, and breathe deeply to commune with Spirits who will reluctantly tell the hidden story, a tale of mystery and surprises. The old woman turns to walk away.

"Come," she snaps.

Jane suddenly realizes what she has just heard.

"What did you say?"

The woman sighs.

"You said 'before she left'. You mean before she – died," Jane insists.

"I say what I mean," says the Wise Woman.

Jane feels her head spinning. She looks around wildly; stares at Sandeep, looking for reassurance that she isn't mad.

"So she isn't dead?" she whispers.

The old woman looks at her – quite gently for once.

"I don't know what she is now," she says. "But she was not dead when she left the village. India was too much for her. Poor little white thing. She couldn't live here." She almost spits, but not quite. "You, too. You'll soon be gone, English Lady," she adds.

"No!" cries Jane. "This is my home. Where would I go? Why do you say that?"

Sandeep speaks first. There's surprise in his voice.

"Of course you know. You are to be sent to England. Everyone knows."

But it's a shock to Jane. Nobody has said anything to her.

"*I* don't know. And my mother ... my father always said she was ..."

"Go ask him now. Ask about his *feringhi* lies."

THE HOUSE

But now, look up from the stream across the foggy green lawn to see the house – at least, you think it's a house. It's a space of shadow, drifting; is it there, or is it not? Walk with me across the little bridge – it's a toy bridge in a toy wilderness – across the grass which becomes smoother as we approach the shadow, which does, yes, resolve itself into solidity. A house, then. In a country half a world away from Suri's cave. A noise. Step back behind the tree. Something moves near the wall of an outbuilding – someone is chopping wood. So there is life in the great shadowy house.

Be a shadow, too. Come with me to the window. Behind us that long, grey-green lawn. The trees where we were standing now themselves almost erased – as if someone has changed their mind in drawing the view and smudged half the world.

Even through the window you sense a shortness of temper – and breath – in the exchange that's unravelling before you in the room. But we don't have to stay out in the chill. Mind you stay close to me behind the curtain.

The old man sits at his breakfast and angrily waves a letter – we guess it's a letter – at the thin, black-clad servant – we guess he's a servant. The old man is not happy. His face is bright red – though we don't know whether from outrage or if this is its natural state. His voice is raised.

"Girl! What do I know of girls? My brother-in-law has turned mad as we always knew he would. It's to be expected in India. What do we know of girls here?"

The tall, thin man in black speaks. It's the sound you imagine the trees behind us might make if the wind were to rise just a little bit to disturb the silent mist. A tapping together of twigs and a surrounding breath. He opines that Mrs. Pitcher had once been a girl.

"Harrumph." The paper slams down on to the plate of scrambled egg.

"Do I understand the girl is to come here?" whispers – it's time we gave him his name – whispers Darkling.

"My brother considers she needs to be schooled and civilized," snorts the General. "Until the school is found, she is to come here."

"It will be company ..." He has no chance to finish.

"Company! What can we do with company? There will be tears and regrets. Mark what I say." The General devotes his attention once more to his breakfast. Darkling sighs from the room.

These are the times before the telegraph or even the railways, when most people travel no further from home than they can walk and only the rich have horses or can afford the fare on the coaches that run from town to town – bumpily, and very slowly, both in winter when the roads turn to soup, and in summer when hardened ruts break wheels and axles. In these times a letter between towns can take days, and between countries might take months. And an answer as many more. So we will need to make use of our time machine to return to the hot springtime in India as this letter is written.

THE LETTER

And now, with the doors of his study open to the shade of the veranda, her father is writing the letter he will send to England, and whose reading you have seen. Several times in the past weeks he has been uncharacteristically angry with his beloved daughter, and he is sorry.

The anger comes from worry and from the knowledge of his own inadequacy. He doesn't know how to bring her through the next stage of her life, how to help her change from the happy wild thing she is into the young woman – the young lady – that she must become.

Her life prospects are difficult enough as it is. She has grown up far from her own kind – an outpost of a few foreigners in a country they love, but thousands of miles from the world where they belong. Even though he has chosen this life for himself, he feels he has to give her the chance to take a place in society if she chooses.

So he has decided, with a great deal of heartache, that the only way to achieve this for her is to send her to his dear lost wife's brother in England, and for him – the General – to arrange for Jane's schooling. And so he writes, with a heavy feeling in his stomach – a feeling that he is betraying his dearest friend, his daughter.

Jane attempts to sneak back to her bedroom, as she has successfully done so often in the past. But her father is listening for her and calls her into his study.

"You are going to England. It's time you were tamed and taught something about being a young lady," he tells her. He tries to sound gentle, but there's an unusual edge to his voice. For the first time in her life, there will be no discussion. "I have sent a letter to your mother's brother."

"I know," she says. "Everyone knows except me."

He looks at her strangely. "I have only this morning decided – after your antics of last night, my girl."

"Well, everyone knows. And something else they know." Her voice shakes as she clutches the brooch in her hand. His eyebrows rise.

"You said mother was dead. But she isn't. She's in England, and I'm going to find her."

His familiar face drains of its colour. He looks himself like the ghost he must be seeing.

"What do you mean?"

She opens her hand and shows him the brooch. He reaches out, but she closes her fist around it and draws her hand back to her side. He stares at her for a long while. "Everyone knows except me," she says again.

He looks at her face for the longest while. "My little girl," he says.

"Hers, too," she says.

"Yes, but she left us." He draws her to him. "You're old enough now. Tomorrow I'll tell you the whole story – short and sad though it is. Yes, she might still live. I don't know where she is. She left us because she was not made for India, and I think it drove her a little bit mad here."

"She went back to England?"

"She went to England; but I don't know any more than that. We'll talk more this evening when I return."

But it was not to be.

We'll go with him, leaving Jane-no-longer-to-be-Suri to catch up on her sleep. Their village lies in the corn-lands of India's northwest; and this is the time before the tentacles of the British have reached this far. When he first came, he was an exotic stranger seeking escape from his own kind. Now he is less strange, but the British soldiers of the Company are coming closer, and so all *feringhi* are mistrusted, however well-loved by a few.

Jane's father rides to Amritsar. There, in an alley not far from the Golden Temple, near the park called the Jallianwala Bagh, where in a little more than a hundred years' time British soldiers will massacre hundreds of innocent people, there the story of Jane's father ends. The people who kill him are right to be suspicious of the British. But they are wrong to believe that all *feringhi* are the same.

Luckily – if that can be said – Jane's father had not yet arrived at the house of his friend, who begins to search for him once he is a few hours late (this is India, where punctuality is not prized or even desirable). So it's not long – only the next morning – before Jane hears what has happened.

"Why?" is all she can scream. "What had he done?"

"Not what he did but what he is," says Sandeep.

"And you, too," says the housekeeper. "You must go to England."

"I don't know anyone in England. Everything I know is here. This is my home."

But they persuade her that she has to go, as her father had wished.

"I'll come back," she says. "When I'm older."

And they say yes, even though they don't believe it, for what else can they say?

"And I'll find my mother," she says.

And they nod and hug her and wish her luck; and the older ones who remember her mother's brief time in the village keep their doubts to themselves.

And so her ship rides a great wave of hopes, fears, and expectations all the way to England.

PART ONE – NOW

THE MESSAGE

London. The greatest seaport of the country. Where Jane takes her first shaky steps onto English soil after so many months at sea – where she staggers and wobbles like a new-born colt across the cobbled surface of the dockside, because the ground moves so much and won't keep still.

She has not been alone on the ship. Other people disembark, too, each of them with their own life and their own purposes. And one or two of their threads are woven through the story of Jane's life; though she will never know them.

The ship has docked – she has worked her way from the Atlantic, through the

Channel, passing between Margate and Southend and up the river with the smell of home all around her. The ship's occupants now have new sights to see – where for weeks the only entertainment has been each other. Now they see people on the shore, passing up and down on foot, or with carts, or (those who can afford it) on horseback.

The sailors begin to feel the familiar mix of joy to be safely home and dread of being trapped. Already they half wish they could turn around and sail in the other direction, back to the open seas. Not so the passengers, who are simply glad to arrive at last.

Jane has talked to many people on the ship. Her fate and the reasons for her journey are no secret.

And yet something gives her an uneasy feeling as she notices a small man in a dark coat pushing through the throngs of dockers, sailors, passengers and their greeting families on the dockside. She is sure she would have noticed him if he'd been a fellow traveller; yet he came from the ship. She has no reason to think of him twice, yet she feels a stab of fear, and can't explain why. And then, in the hustle and worry of getting herself on the road to her uncle – for she left India so soon after her father's death that no letter would have travelled faster, and nobody is here to meet her or knows she was coming – in all that worry and difficulty for a fourteen-year-old girl on her own, she quickly forgets the man she briefly thought of as the Raven.

But he has not forgotten Jane, and you are privileged as she is not, to see where he goes. Clear of the dockyard carts and crowds, he throws a small boy a farthing to fetch him a cab; and he rides to the other side of London, beyond St. Paul's, over the Fleet bridge and into Fleet Street, where he pays the driver and disappears northward into the alleys around the Inns of Court.

In the corner of a tiny courtyard, if you look hard enough, you will see the entrance to a staircase, and painted on a small board are the names of the inhabitants. The Raven does not pause to read them, since he has been here often before, and is well acquainted with Mr. Theophilus Hardfist, attorney at law, and somewhat down on his luck – into whose rooms he bursts without announcement.

"He's dead. Killed by a band of Sikh murderers," says the Raven.

"Oh, dear," replies Hardfist, with no great excess of surprise. "A band ... Were they expensive?"

"There's a great distrust of the English in the Punjab. They believe the British want to take over their kingdom. A fatal result – should such be desired – might require no more than a gentle nudge. "

"So everything now goes to the girl ..." Hardfist muses, with some satisfaction. The Raven, knowing that no response is required of him, stands waiting for instruction. Hardfist strolls reflectively across his threadbare carpet and peers out of the grimy window into his sorry yard. From watching him you would have thought he was striding across a great salon to examine his estate. A mouse skitters across the room and disappears through a hole beside the cold fireplace. Hardfist turns. "I shall inform her myself, I think," he says.

But it's not Jane he is talking of.

He begins to smooth down what remains of his short, dark hair, and to pull straight the wayward buttons of his shirt. He has already forgotten the presence of the man we know as the Raven. He takes his coat from the back of the door and his stick from the corner. Without a further glance at his room he descends the stairs, crosses the yard, and – once he has emerged from the narrow alleys – disappears in the heavy traffic along the Holborn.

He dodges in and out among the walking crowds, the carts, cabs, carriages, and cabbages, and turns down another alley towards Covent Garden. He looks around to be sure that nobody is following before he continues to the area of Seven Dials. In these streets he is rare as a peacock – a man whose coat is scarcely threadbare, and whose shoes still protect his feet from the water of the gutter. Everywhere he looks, he meets hostile stares, but he is undisturbed. He knows where he is going – and he knows he can protect himself if the need should arise. He squeezes past the children on the doorstep and climbs the creaking stairs of a house in Monmouth Street. Four flights up, he knocks on a door.

"Wild! 'Tis Hardfist."

There's a movement in the room, but the door remains shut.

"I've a two-guinea task for you."

After a minute or two, the door opens a crack. Hardfist taps his foot impatiently. "Come on, Wild. I'll see you swing for sure, but it won't be today."

The man Wild is surprisingly young, good-looking, and well-dressed for the streets in which we find him. It might be that his suspicion of callers comes from a fear of being discovered. In short, he may be hiding from something, or somebody. Still, he knows Hardfist, and opens the door wide enough for the lawyer to enter the room. He gestures to the chair, but Hardfist shakes his head.

"No time for that, I thank you." Hardfist speaks crisply. "There's a girl on her way to Wiltshire, and I require you to be there. Find her. Keep apart from her, but always be aware of what she is doing. I'll send instructions in a day or two."

With a few more rapid details, Hardfist turns to go. Quick as a snake, Wild's hand snaps to grip the lawyer's arm.

Hardfist's face softens into the semblance of a smile. He draws a guinea from his pocket and hands the coin to Wild. The grip loosens not a jot until, after several reluctant seconds, the second promised guinea joins its brother. So the chase is started.

HIGHWAYMAN

"Mutton chops! Excellent. You know, James, sometimes I feel I could kill for a good mutton chop. Or die. One or the other."

"I feel you might notice the difference, my dear General." And James roars with loud laughter.

"Not at all, since if I were not enjoying my chop, I should be dead and past knowing anything at all. "

Something tickles a memory in the cellars of James's mind.

"Well, George," for such is the General's name, "what will you do about this little Indian girl?"

"Indian girl?" The General jumps as if somebody has goosed him.

"Your sister's child."

"What will I do? Gracious, nothing, of course. I know nothing about children – most of all girl children. A boy might have been different. At least I was a boy myself once." And he laughs with great enjoyment while his friend smiles politely. The General continues, "I fancy if I keep quiet then the whole idea will simply slip away. That's my belief."

"And your most religious hope." James laughs until he is quite pink in the face.

Be kind to them. They may seem a pair of ignorant grotesques, but they mean well and never wish harm to anyone. Also, they're about to have something of a shock as the little girl in question is not very far away.

You remember the letter, of course, and the General's reaction before he squished it into his scrambled egg. It's good that someone remembers, because now, not two weeks after the excitements of that morning, the General has entirely forgotten the occasion.

The General is a very gregarious person. He loves nothing better than to spend his evenings surrounded by his friends, talking – and also drinking. Especially drinking – a lot. Of course, he doesn't think it's a lot because he has no money troubles and because he does it all the time. But you would be astonished by the amount he could put down on a daily basis and still remain upright, able to move, and apparently able to function quite normally.

It's a pity for him – and also for his friends, because he's a very generous man and they share in everything that he does – that he is wrong about the money. He has drunk his way through a small fortune over the years, and a small fortune was all he had. So there's a bit of a storm cloud building over the General's life, but for now he's too interested in his friends and the bottle in front of him to notice it.

"I say, James. It's awful dull here. What do you say to a little canter to blow out some cobwebs?" (When the General says *canter*, he means gallop as fast as the poor horse can manage, and much too fast to be safe.)

"Excellent!" James is an enthusiastic horseman, and never misses the chance to beat up the countryside. (Imagine what he could have done on a motorbike. Sadly, he will die in a riding accident seventy-five years before a suitable motorbike is invented. He will ride too fast and too carelessly and his horse will stumble and throw him. His neck will break in a millisecond, and that will be the end of James.

But that's not yet, and not this afternoon.)

"Clears the old attic, what?" the General shouts above the thudding of hoof on turf as they gallop across the hill. "I feel younger already."

They arrive at the ridge from which they can look down on the road that snakes its rambling way through the valley below. The road precisely follows the winding, shallow, shambling river, since the locals have never stirred themselves to build any bridges to shorten the way. Consequently, journeys along the valley are slow. Prime country for highwaymen, in fact. And this is the thought that occurs to the General as he looks down on the slow-moving coach struggling along the road.

"Fancy a game, James?" he says, a wide grin on his face.

"Always," says James.

"A dull thing, travelling by coach," says the General. "Let's give those lucky passengers a bit of excitement. Brighten their day. Sure to be grateful."

And the General pulls his kerchief up to cover the bottom of his pink face. In a flash, an observer would say he resembled nothing so much as the good old General with a kerchief over his face. But his friend is not one to spoil an enthusiasm.

"Capital!" he yelps with joy, and pulls up his own kerchief in similar fashion.

"Tally ho!" shouts the General.

"View halloo!" adds James. And they launch themselves down the hill towards the innocent carriage.

As you have guessed, this is the very carriage in which Jane is travelling. She's looking eagerly out of the window, thinking to herself, "This is my home now. What a lovely little valley. And so green. And my mother ... maybe I'll see her again soon."

And so she is the first to see the galloping horsemen advancing on the coach, and soon the riders are close enough for her to see the kerchiefs on their faces and one word floods her mind.

"Highwaymen!" she cries out.

The young man leans suddenly forward, pushing her aside to see for himself. She notices with surprise and a little admiration that he doesn't appear disturbed – indeed, almost the opposite, as a satisfied smile seems to play about his lips.

"Excellent," he says, and leans back again.

He's a dark and handsome young man and has a way of lounging as if he's at home, even in this tight space – and for some reason he has never removed his right hand from his coat pocket. What could be the solution to that mystery?

(Her journey has been full of mysteries. She has kept herself sane by looking at the people around her, and thinking, *What secrets lie under that hat, or behind those walls?* though she never finds out the answer.)

But now she is frightened. She has heard stories of highwaymen. In the stories, the highwaymen are always noble and handsome and treat ladies well. Though they might gently remove their jewels, some short while later they will return them secretly, having fallen in love with the lady they have robbed.

She has no experience to tell how closely this might resemble real life, but at this moment, with two masked men approaching at speed, and her coach defenceless on a narrow road, she loses her confidence in romances. She thinks that most likely she will be hurt or killed. And in any case, she will be robbed and lose everything – and Lord knows, she has brought little enough with her from India.

The coach has pulled to a halt.

"Out of the carriage, ladies and gentlemen!" a voice thunders from outside.

Jane is the first out. She has to look up to see the highwayman. The horse is large, and the sky bright, even though there is no sun. She sees nothing but a towering black shape, and what she takes to be an impatiently waggling pistol.

A strange thing has happened to James and the General on their way down the hill. At the top, as they pull up their kerchiefs, they intend nothing more than a good wild ride to stop the coach, followed by a hearty round of laughter and possibly some apologetic drinking.

But as the ride becomes wilder, and faster; as they come close enough to see the fear on the coachmen's faces, something changes in them. The disguise they wear has become the real thing. And now the coach has stopped and they have ordered the occupants out on the road, even though they have no real intention of robbing or harming anyone, who can tell the difference between them and real highway robbers? And perhaps there is none. It's a dangerous game. Much more dangerous than they had wanted or expected. As they are about to find out.

PISTOL

Jane turns to see the thin man helping the flustered lady from the carriage. There's a loud bang – a pistol shot. The flustered lady shrieks and faints dead away. The thin man tries valiantly to hold her up, but is dragged down by her not inconsiderable weight.

"I have two pistols. The other is still loaded," says the young man as he appears around the rear end of the coach. But he is talking to the air. The General, it's true, required a moment to recover from the shock, but now he and his friend are turned and galloping away without a backward glance. The young man aims his pistol carefully and fires at the retreating highwaymen, but it's too far even for such an expert shot as he. Of course, he knows that very well, and if you thought his aim was not to hit a highwayman but to impress a young lady, you might not be wrong.

"So. Let us continue our journey," he says, and holds his hand out to Jane, helping her to her seat in the coach before turning to the assistance of the thin man and some rather heavier lifting.

At last Jane steps down from the coach in the yard of the village inn. Now all that remains of her journey is the road from the village to the Priory and her mother's brother.

"I wonder what he will be like," she says to herself.

The young man smiles. "Shall I see you again?"

"I fear it unlikely. I go no further," she says.

"But I, too, will be staying a while," he says, a broad grin lighting up his face.

"Well, then, perhaps we shall meet again. Thank you, sir." Suddenly she is all maidenly modesty.

"It was a privilege to be of service," he says. "I hope that our paths will indeed cross before too long." He takes her hand and bows over it – not quite daring to kiss her fingers.

"Until then, sir," she smiles at him, and turns away.

She may have need of him in the future, because Robert Wild, messenger of Hardfist, the lawyer, is not far away now.

And what are the General and his faithful James doing while all this is going on? If you were to look around the corner into the stables of the inn yard, you might see that two of the horses seem familiar. And now James and the General sit in the dark corner of the inn's main room, making themselves comfortable in the alcove next to the chimney, where the brightness of the fire makes the shadow around them that much stronger. It has not been long since their adventure, but the jug of wine they've just finished is not their first.

"Capital fun!" exclaims the General.

"Even more excitement than we hoped for!" agrees James. Neither of them is going to admit how terrified they were when the pistol went off.

"Another cup. What do you think, James?"

"Excellent!"

The waiter brings a third jug of wine. "A young lady has set off to your house, General. She's asking for you."

"Young lady? Really? After servant's work?"

"She didn't look like a servant, General."

"Ha!" James explodes with delight, slapping the arm of his chair. "Your niece! The girl from India!" Suddenly he becomes serious. "I say," he says quietly. "You don't think it was the young lady on that coach, do you? Do you think she will remember us?"

The last time the General looked this worried was one afternoon in the Peninsular wars. He feared the surrounding French army might pin them down for days, and that his brother officers would finish the regimental wine before he could be there to assist them.

THE LONGEST NIGHT

Jane travels the last three miles to Nightride Priory – for that is the name of the General's house – in a brand new trap, pulled by a sprightly pony. The innkeeper is very proud of this little carriage. It's brightly painted, and its leather seats still smell of new leather, and its wood of new varnish. The wheels turn without a creak, and the ride is springy and comfortable. A fine vehicle to deliver a pretty lady to the big house, he thinks. But Jane doesn't really notice. She is drinking up every fresh morsel of these last few minutes' journey.

"This is my new home," she is thinking. And, "I wonder if my mother is here?"

At last the little trap clip-clops smoothly up to the big house and stops by the steps to the front door. Jane pulls at the bell. She turns to look at the landscape, smiling at the impatient driver. She turns back to the door. Its paint is peeling, she notices.

Like the General himself, his house is interesting, but crumbling, and parts of it have not been visited in years. A tour guide would tell you that it was originally a priory – so a place dedicated to pure thoughts and good works – until greedy Henry VIII abolished these holy monasteries and took most of their riches for himself. What the guide won't tell you is that by Henry's time the holy company of monks was reduced to a fat abbot and two scrawny but gluttonous companions, who spent their days drinking their way through the vast wine cellar and taking for the priory kitchens the best of everything the local villagers produced. Small wonder that they were kicked out and a large portion of the priory's stones used to improve many of the local houses.

The remainder was turned into a comfortable residence for the General's ancestors. One result of this extensive remodelling was that nobody could keep track of the various cellars, crypts, and passages of the original priory, many of which remained untouched under the ground, giving rise to countless local legends of treasure, ghosts, and vengeance.

And some of these will change the lives of both Jane and the General.

After an age, the door opens. A face

emerges reluctantly from the shadow as the gap widens. It's Darkling, doing his job.

"Madam?"

Lucky that Mrs. Pitcher happens to be passing across the hall. Unlike Darkling, she remembers the letter, and in no time, Jane's few bags are brought in; she's shown the room which will be hers; and Mrs. Pitcher sits her in the green salon while she makes tea and they wait for the General to return.

"How long will he be?" Jane asks. Mrs. Pitcher shrugs and pats her on the shoulder with a smile.

"The General will be here when the General is here," she says. Which reminds Jane of the Wise Woman in the Punjab and makes her feel sad for a few minutes.

"Is my mother not here?" she asks eagerly, as Mrs. Pitcher passes by once again on some mysterious errand. The housekeeper stops dead as if pulled up at the end of a rope.

"Mother?" she says. "Do you mean the General's sister? Oh, no dear, she hasn't been here for many years."

"Well, do you know where she is?"

"Oh, no. Not seen or heard of her since ... well, since she went off with ... I suppose he was your father." But then she remembers she has heard something.

"Wait a minute," she says. Jane's hopes rise. "I thought we heard she was ... she had ..."

"Died," says Jane, sadly.

The day rambles onward. The light thickens in the room. The fire burns brighter. Mrs. Pitcher brings candles – only two, since candles are expensive, and she doesn't yet know how the General feels about his niece. But the General remains insubstantial as a rumour, a figure remarkable only for his absence. Jane is bored to distraction – and becoming jittery with it.

At last she tells Mrs. Pitcher that she would like to go to bed.

Of course she can't sleep. She feels very alone and very orphaned, and desperately wishes herself in India, where she understands life. Where she understands how people think. The time between each tick of the clock lengthens magically to several minutes, and the thought of the weeks and months to come is miserable.

To put it bluntly, the General has been hiding. He is as frightened of the girl as she is of him. And naturally, he has continued his drinking. After a while, even James has had enough.

"Must go. Must go!" he says, and drags the reluctant General into the night air.

It's a fair way from the village to his house – but not nearly as far as the General walks that night (too drunk to remember his horse). Not for the first time on such occasions, he takes a long and complicated path to his door.

So it's long after midnight when he finally arrives. Darkling is ready. The door opens before the General has a chance to ring the bell or thump on the wood. The night is Darkling's realm, and he doesn't mind waiting for the General to come home – something he has done often enough since they were both young men together.

You find it hard to imagine Darkling as a young man? Don't trouble yourself. He was no different. He has looked much the same since he grew to his full height (slightly under six feet), an altitude he reached at the age of thirteen – and even before that day he was but a shorter version of his future self. Darkling has remained more or less unchanged since he could first walk.

It's a silent routine, the General's journey from the front steps to his bed chamber, where, within five minutes of his arrival his snores are ruffling the fringes of his nightcap. The process looks effortless, but that simply conceals Darkling's skill.

So at last the house sleeps.

THE DEVIL'S KIDNEYS

Jane spends a restless night and is glad when rainy daylight finally appears and she can leave her room again. She comes down to find the General in the dining room, alone at a great, long, old-fashioned table. He looks confused to see her, as if he has no idea who she is.

He has no idea who I am, Jane thinks. But his hangover-clouded brain begins to stir.

"Ah, girl! Slept well? Mrs. Pitcher looking after you?"

"Yes, thank you, sir," she says.

"Oh, no need for that. Call me General. Everyone else does." He looks around for some inspiration. "Have a kidney. Devilled. Excellent. Good for the brain." He has no idea whether devilled kidneys are good for the brain or not. He wants to show the girl she's welcome, and he can't think of anything else to say.

But Jane is not yet used to English food, and the thought of something so rich – and so much of it – at breakfast time is too much for her. She takes some bread and milk and sits as far from the

General as she decently can. His fund of conversation is in any case exhausted, and he confines himself to looking across at her during pauses in his eating and drinking to smile and nod encouragingly in her direction.

She plucks up courage to ask about her mother. "I heard my mother was in England," she says. He looks bewildered.

"Mother?"

"Your sister," Jane says, helpfully, and she can see the penny dropping in the rusty mechanism of the General's brain.

"Ah," he says. "Heard she was, er … dead, child. Long time ago. Sorry."

The clock-ticking silence rolls over them again. The tide of time, you might say. It's one of the longest meals Jane has ever known, and ends at last (after fifteen minutes or so) when the General finishes his tea, brushes the crumbs from his whiskers, and shambles out of the room – as glad to be alone again as she is.

Even though the voyage from Bombay was long; even though she was sad that her father was dead, and her childhood was over; even so, all through the voyage there was excitement in thoughts of England and her uncle; something to look forward to. Now all that is over – like Christmas after you've opened all your presents.

But, in spite of it all, she refuses to believe that her mother is dead. She has a tiny, shiny spark of hope. She has the locket. She has the word of the Wise Woman. And somehow, she just knows.

She hasn't been wasting her time. After all, there's more to the house than the rooms she saw in her first few hours. At first she worried that she might be going where she shouldn't. But then she thinks, I'm not afraid of Mrs. Pitcher or that funny old Darkling. I won't do any harm. And she starts a good, thorough exploration. At the back of her mind, there's still the idea that she might discover some clue about the mystery of her mother.

She feels a kind of delicious shock in the afternoon when, out of a side window, she sees the ruined part of the house for the first time. She doesn't understand how a house can be at once grand and falling down. Something very terrible must have happened. She wonders what stories of death and betrayal could have caused this decay and destruction. She's so wrapped in these thoughts that she doesn't hear the soft footsteps approaching behind her. Only when she feels the downy hairs on her neck prickle does she becomes aware that something …

"We don't go in there," a voice whispers very close to her ear. She shrieks and turns, drawing back into the corner away from the window. It's Darkling. A single tooth protrudes through a small and slightly triumphant smile on his face. "It's dangerous in the ruins," he adds. "Best to stay away." She imagines a departing spirit might haunt these corridors and its voice would whisper in just this way: as the draught from a closing door disturbs a discarded letter.

"Why is it dangerous?"

His smile broadens to reveal a second tooth. "Best to stay away." He's gone like the last breath of a dying day, and the shadows fall across the corridor behind him as she stands in the failing light of the window, and soon in the dusk is unable to see the ruins any longer.

TWINS

The next morning is dull and windy, but the constant rain has stopped – for a while at least – leaving only a suspicion of drizzle in the air. With a sense of sudden freedom, Jane steps from the house and into the refreshing air. She soon sees that the house she knows from the inside doesn't so much stop as slowly fade away. Over there is a room with no windows. Here's one with no roof. There a floor protruding from a broken turret clinging to the upper half of a wall, the lower twenty feet fallen away to rubble. The gradual collapse continues over twenty or thirty metres before finally only a few low walls show the outline of the great priory that once was. But look here ... a door. She tries the handle. Naturally, it's locked.

"It's locked," a cheerful voice informs her. "We've tried lots of times."

Startled, Jane looks round. On the other side of the fence which marks the edge of the Priory's home garden stands a friendly girl of around her own age, and a similar boy. In fact, he is so similar Jane thinks they can only be twins.

"We're the twins," says the girl.

"We live in the village," the boy adds.

"But we come here a lot, because …" the girl begins. "… we like solving mysteries," her brother finishes. Jane laughs. "I suppose you always …"

"Finish each other's sentences," they say together. "Yes."

"We do," the boy adds.

"Because he always has to have the last word," his sister says.

"What mysteries?" says Jane.

"There are so many." "We don't know where to begin," they say between them.

She encourages them to begin wherever they like, and they walk around the ruins and the house together, while the twins point out the places where so many fabulous things supposedly happened, and where a headless monk walks chanting through the fallen nave of the priory church at full moon.

"Only one?" asks Jane.

"Not always," they say. Lights have been seen high up at the windows of roofless rooms. "And there's a woman screaming – crying for help. They say she's the mad sister of the old General. He locks her up because he can't let her out to wander the world in her madness."

Jane shudders. "My mother is the General's sister," she says, very quietly.

"We know …"

"It's not true. I don't want to hear any more," Jane says. "I think I hear Mrs. Pitcher calling …"

"We'll come back tomorrow," they shout after her. "We'll show you our house. We've got a secret passage …"

She's shaken and excited by what she's heard – and she doesn't know whether she likes these twins. She resolves to sit the General down and make him talk to her properly. She has hardly seen him since she arrived. It's almost as if he were avoiding her. Well, that has to stop.

"You have to go home sometime, General, old friend," says James, as the General calls for another jug of wine. "You can't keep stayin' out of her way."

"I know," says the General. "She's

only a young gel," says James, encouragingly. "Won't bite or bark."

"It all looks very simple to you, I dare say," grumps the General. "But let me tell you, if she were a tiny child it would be easy. You just treat 'em like puppies and leave 'em to Mrs. Pitcher. And if she were a grown woman – well, no doubt she'd be on her way soon. But she's neither fish nor fowl, and if I'm honest I have to admit I'm at something of a loss."

"I'd never have guessed, old man," James says drily. "But listen – you're not frightened of Boney. You wouldn't want the world to know you're afraid of a young gel."

"No," says the General thoughtfully. "Ah well, I suppose there's nothing for it." He drains his mug of wine and races out of the door – quick, before his mind can change itself. Quick, to meet whatever fate might have in store for him at his own home, now become strange …

COURAGE OF THE GENERAL

Evening has fallen once more at Nightride Priory. Jane has insisted that she and the General sit together, and here they are, looking up from the fire and smiling encouragingly at one another from time to time. Jane doesn't know how to start a conversation, and the General is wondering what to say to this creature and what will happen if he does bring himself to speak. The clock chimes another quarter. The fire cracks. The General takes his courage firmly in both hands.

"How are you getting on, my dear?" he asks.

"I met the twins today," says Jane. The General is mystified. "Twins?"

"From the village. My age …"

"Ah. Children. I knew their mother, you know."

"Do you see much of her?" Jane immediately thinks of a romantic attachment, since she doesn't know anything about the twins' father.

"Haven't seen her in years. Pretty young thing … Yes, indeed. Pretty young thing."

His voice fades. Conversation dries again. A log falls in the fire. Darkling brings in the General's after-dinner port, and the application of a glass of this medicine does wonders for the General's powers of conversation.

"I suppose we'll have to send you away," he says to Jane – the thought is something of a relief to him.

"Why?"

"For educating. Can't have you moping around here forgetting things. You need to be fitted for something."

"Isn't marriage the only thing a young woman can be fitted for?" says Jane, a little mischievously – but the General doesn't notice.

"And how are you going to be married if you hide away here and talk to no one, eh? Well, my girl?"

Jane has no answer, but a weight seems to settle in her stomach. What does she really have to look forward to? She has no fortune, no education, nothing in the world but her native intelligence and an amount of prettiness. At that moment, life does not seem to promise a great deal. She gets up from her chair.

"I think I shall go to bed," she says.

The General nods.

"Excellent notion. Sleep well, my girl," he says.

Of course she can't sleep. She puts out her candle and lies first on her back, then on one side, and then the other, turning as if on a spit, she thinks. The moon is bright. The light forces its way through a gap in the heavy curtains, and – as the world turns – the shaft of light travels across the wall, and over her bed until it strikes her squarely in the face. At this point she gives up her pretence of sleep and climbs out of bed. She hears a clock strike a single note, which tells her very little, since it does that on each quarter-hour.

She creeps out along the corridor to the window at the far end, from where she can look down on the moonlit ruins. She has no particular aim in mind, she just likes the mystery of the moonlit scene. But look, now. Is that a shadow she sees flitting amongst the stones?

An owl lands on the crumbling wall and peers beakily around.

But that shadow, there … surely it

moved. And there ... the flickering of a lamp, quickly extinguished as its bearer emerges from the ruin into the moonlight. Jane's heart is thumping. A hooded figure makes its way slowly across the grass and disappears among the trees.

She determines to find out what's going on.

"I'm not a timid little English girly," she mutters to herself. She runs silent as a mouse to her room to collect her shoes and a cloak – something she had no need of during her childhood in India – and goes as swiftly as she dares down the stairs to the courtyard door of the kitchen passage, which she knows is not as fearsomely locked and bolted as the front door. It's also further from anybody's hearing.

She runs across the courtyard and out to the ruins where she saw the figure in the moonlight. Cautiously, she creeps around the corner of the fallen-down wall to see the open space still flooded with the cold light of the moon. Empty. She looks carefully around her but sees nothing and nobody. Slowly she creeps onward until she reaches the opening where she is sure she saw the figure emerge. But there's nothing here, either.

Suddenly two strong arms grab her from behind. She struggles and kicks, but her attacker is strong and her wriggling makes no impression.

"Let me go!" she shrieks.

"Quiet, or you're dead meat," a voice whispers roughly in her ear.

Not far away, the General is snoring. Gradually his snores increase in volume, until he produces an extra-loud snort and wakes himself up.

However many times he tells the story, he insists that he has no idea what made him get out of bed and look out of his window. Even though there was nothing but the moonlit lawn to see, he felt uneasy, he would later say. He puts on his gown and shoes, picks up a stout walking stick and goes outside.

Jane has struggled and fought and tried to bite, but the arms remain fast around her until it occurs to her to try slipping down inside the too-big cloak, which she has not fastened around her neck. Her assailant is surprised. She manages to kick against him and wriggle her way free and is on her feet before he can regain his balance. At that moment he catches sight of the General, approaching with this stout stick, and he flees.

"Blackguard," cries the General. "Come to rob us! Take that!" and he raises the stick. Only then does he notice Jane looking up at him.

"Jane, my gel! What on earth are you doin' out here?"

The attacker has gone. She tries to explain, but the General doesn't understand.

"Too wild for me," he shakes his head. "Too wild for me ..."

He brings her inside and sees her to her room before returning to his own. His night continues with warlike dreams and battles won. Jane is kept awake until the dawn by a single, nagging thought – did the attacker know who she was? And if he did, what did he want with her?

The next morning Jane walks around the house as if she'd been drugged with laudanum. (Laudanum, as you know, is a popular and freely available medicine made from a mixture of alcohol and opium. It certainly helps take away some of life's pain, but does not greatly improve coordination of thought or movement.) Mrs. Pitcher bustles from the kitchen corridor to find her standing clueless in the doorway.

"Look at you," she says. "Little lost lamb." She sees at once that Jane needs something to do. "Come down here with me and I'll give you a cup of tea and something to do with your hands." Jane follows her meekly, just as the General comes from the dining room, having finished his breakfast.

"Ah, gel. Recovered from your adventure, I trust?"

Jane nods. "Good, very good," says the General. "Must get you away from here before it happens again." And before her tired mind can react to what she's just heard, he is away. "Wonderful morning for a ride," he says. And Jane thinks she might be about to cry. She doesn't want to be homeless again.

CAVENDISH SQUARE

Let's make our way back in time a little and return to London. Hardfist has sent Robert Wild to search for Jane and now continues his walk from the rookeries of St. Giles, where people go to disappear – whether that is their intention or not – to the town houses of Cavendish Square, where those people live who wish to be seen.

It's a walk of ten minutes or so, yet, as so often in London – even in our own days – the boundary between having too much and having nothing at all can be crossed by going from one side of the road to the other.

It's a pleasant square, with gardens in the centre for the private enjoyment of its inhabitants, who were originally the rich and noble. Since then the fortunes of the square have declined a little, but not altogether. Horatio Lord Nelson lived here with his wife not so long ago, and the square will never fall so far as to resemble the slums of the once-grand St. Martin's Lane through which Hardfist has recently walked.

The lawyer Hardfist steps up to a front door and pulls to ring the bell. The footman knows him, and he enters without ceremony to wait in a drawing room on the first floor.

It's a grand room for a town house, and, coming here for the first time, you would most likely be impressed and wish you could live here yourself. But look a little harder. The carpet is faded. The ornate plaster decoration around the edge of the ceiling and around the candelabrum is chipped in places and needs re-painting entirely. The chairs would certainly benefit from attention to their upholstery. But in spite of these details, the overall effect is grand enough to convince a casual visitor. Appearances are kept up.

The door opens. Hardfist turns to greet an imposing woman in her sixties as she enters the room. She doesn't speak, but waits for him to announce the purpose of his visit.

"The daughter has returned to England," he says.

"And?"

"And I believe I know where she is."

"And?"

"I believe I can bring her to you. She is but fourteen years old and will require a guardian."

"What do I want with a child about my neck?"

Hardfist is irritated. He had expected a greater understanding and – crucially – more applause for his efforts. "With her father's brother no longer with us, her father inherited, whether he wished it or not. And now …"

"Ah." The lady relaxes. She begins to understand. No further words are necessary. Hardfist returns to his office and writes a letter, which he sends to Wiltshire by the next coach.

AN EDUCATION

Jane needs to escape from the house and calm her fears of being sent away. She puts on her bonnet and cape (both still unfamiliar and awkward) and walks to the village in the hope of meeting someone – anyone. The locals are not yet used to her – though of course everyone knows who she is – and the few people she passes on the road or who watch from the fields nod in a friendly manner and stare after her, but say nothing. She is relieved to see the twins coming from their house close by the church.

"I'm to be sent away," she blurts out before they have a chance to speak.

"Why?" they say in chorus.

"To school somewhere." They laugh, which upsets her. "It's not funny," she says, hurt.

"We don't think it's funny at all. It's just nothing to cry about." Jane looks blank. "We have a governess who teaches us. You simply come to our house for your school," they say between them.

A wave of relief and happiness makes Jane give out a great laugh – a happy burp. "Then the problem is gone!" she says.

But life doesn't usually turn out to be that simple.

They walk through the village and across the winter fields. The twins are enthralled and impressed to hear of the attack in the night. They laugh with glee at the General's bravery. We would never have thought it, they say. And wonder who the strange attacker could be.

Walking and chatting happily, they arrive at the edge of a copse on a hill above the village.

And suddenly it's as if night has fallen. A man on a great dark horse thunders along the track from behind the trees. Surprised by Jane and the twins, the horse rears up and whinnies, a glooming dark shape above them, silhouetted against the scudding grey clouds. The wind whips a sharp skein of drizzle across their faces. They cry out in surprise, which startles the horse again, and it wheels around, its rider struggling to stay in control. At last he has the horse firmly in his hands again.

"Stupid children!" he barks at them, before turning his horse around and galloping away across the hill.

The twins laugh in surprise and relief. "What a fool," they agree. But Jane's face is grey as the clouds.

"It was him," she says. "It was him. It was his voice. He's still here."

BLACKMAIL

Leave Jane and the twins to find their way home. They will go to the twins' house and drink comforting tea with muffins they toast at the fire because that's what they like. They will talk of everything and nothing, as people do as they learn to know each other.

But you will want to return with me to Nightride Priory, because that is where the man on the black horse is going – and his message will not be welcome.

It's the General's bad luck that he happens to be on his way out and walking down the steps of his house as the rider approaches. This means that he is unable to pretend that he is not at home.

"General." The rider touches his hat as he reins in his horse – a magnificent and no doubt expensive animal, the General notices with approval – and a certain amount of envy. The General nods and makes as if to continue his walk, leaving the care of this stranger to his servants.

"It is you that I have come to see, General," says the rider. "Is the time not convenient?" Now, the General is suspicious of any unannounced visit and feels unprepared. "If you wish to speak to me, I would rather it were tomorrow," he says.

"As you wish, but tomorrow may be too late."

The General senses (correctly) that something unpleasant is about to happen, and that he will remember the decision he makes now for a long time to come. He looks around.

"I can give my message while you stand here, or while you are seated in comfort in your house. It's all the same to me." The horse begins to move its feet impatiently. A true thoroughbred, it becomes bored easily and doesn't like standing still for long. Still the General is undecided.

"Perhaps you remember the affair of the Lady and the Burgundy," says the stranger, helpfully. The General jumps physically backwards. The rider smiles. "I see you do," he says. The General turns without a further word and returns to the house, leaving the rider to dismount and follow.

The General has taken advantage of the intervening few seconds to gather his thoughts, and inside, on his own territory, he is brusque. He indicates that the rider should sit, while he remains standing by the fireplace.

"What do you want?" he barks. The rider is not intimidated. He smiles gently.

"I think we will both find that we have something to trade and we can come out of the arrangement satisfied," he says. The General harrumphs and begins to look miserable. What is said over the following five minutes is something the General wants to keep from even his closest friends. It affects him badly, so that to his friend James he seems to have been beaten thin – a shadow of the person he was. You expect to be told, of course, but you will be disappointed for the time being. If the very mention of the Lady and the Burgundy can have such an effect on the General, then how can I treat him so badly as to betray his secret to you?

For the time being, I can say that the General has been human. The twin pressures of past secrets and present lack of money have forced him into a situation which makes him deeply unhappy – and which will shortly lead to new troubles for Jane, too.

REAP THE WHIRLWIND

An hour later finds the General in the inn with his friend James. The General is already well into his second pint of wine as James arrives, summoned by a potboy sent while the General concentrated on consuming the first. James is shocked by his friend's appearance.

"I say, you're not looking at all …"

"It's catching up with me."

"Not the business with …?"

The General nods, sadly. In a little over a hundred years' time, his expression will reappear on the face of a donkey in a wood in Sussex – a creature called Eeyore.

A little later, in the bright, cold sunlight, Jane walks from her friends' house back to Nightride Priory. She's much happier now and beginning to feel that this village is her home. She looks around at the fields and the woods, and the comfortable houses that seem to grow from the landscape, and she sighs happily. As she approaches the house, she hears the sound of a horse and carriage behind her and moves aside to let it pass.

She can't help giving out a frightened squeak when she sees the rider on the black horse beside the little closed carriage. He smiles down at her from the saddle.

"Milady," he says. He springs to the ground and holds open the carriage door. Jane pushes past him, running for the safety of the house, but he grabs her arm. "I'm pleased to say that we'll be companions on a journey," he says. "We're going to London – to see your mother."

Jane gasps and briefly stops her struggling. The door of the house opens, and Darkling drags Jane's trunk out onto the steps, assisted by a puffing Mistress Pitcher. Jane is completely confused. Of course she wants to see her mother, but why is there a feeling of dread in her stomach? *This isn't right,* something is screaming at her and she struggles again.

Behind her she sees the General walking slowly towards the house, his eyes fixed on the gravel of the drive.

"General," Jane screams, "Uncle!"

The General stops and lifts his head to stare blankly at her. It's almost as if he were blind. And seeing the defeated, deflated old man – for he suddenly seems to be much older than she had thought before – Jane feels the fight drain away from her. Nothing is so unwanted as the toys you once loved and are now too old to play with; and so, feeling herself thrown aside like last year's rag doll, Jane allows herself to be pushed into the carriage.

PART TWO

LONDON PARTICULAR

"London is much too big and busy a city for a young girl to be allowed to wander unsupervised. I'm sure you realize that we mean this for the best, my dear. Remember that, however much you might dislike it, I am considerably older, and a little wiser than you and I am *always* looking after your best interests. Never doubt that for a second." She *says* that she is Jane's grandmother. To Jane she's a fierce old woman and she doesn't trust her. She has never before seen anyone quite like her. Now the woman is staring hard at her as if to hammer home her message and ensure that it can never emerge again from behind Jane's eyes.

The parts of London that Jane has seen on her journey from the country to this house in Cavendish Square don't seem at all frightening. She spent much of her childhood in Amritsar, so crowded streets full of children and animals are familiar and reassuring, and not at all alarming. Nevertheless, she lowers her eyes submissively – she, too, can play the game of deceit.

"Yes," she says.

"Yes ... what?"

"Yes, Grandmother."

"Excellent. So you see that by far the best and most sensible course of action is that you remain in this house at all times, save when I am able to accompany you."

She was a prisoner, then. But why? Why was she kidnapped from her uncle's house in the country and brought to London to be locked up with this ... this gorgon? She looks down at the fireplace. Sure enough – the marble figure of a cat. Doubtless the gorgon had glanced into its eyes and it had turned at once to stone. Jane smiles a secret smile.

"Something amuses you ..."

How clever, Jane thinks, *to be able*

to speak a command and a question in one breath. She shakes her head, meekly. "Not at all, Grandmother," she says.

"Very well. I'm sure you would like to make yourself at home in your room. You may borrow any book from the library. You can read, can't you?"

She has a sudden memory: she sits in the shade of the tree by their house in the village, her father giving the daily reading lesson. She can feel the heat, hear the children playing, and the dogs bark. She swallows the lump in her throat.

"Yes, Grandmother. Thank you."

"You will come down for meals, and we shall be able to talk." Her grandmother attempts a smile.

"When shall I see my mother?"

Her grandmother looks stern. "Your mother is away from town for a time. You will see her when she returns."

Jane is dismissed and climbs the stairs to her room on the third floor among the servants. She sits on her little bed – and, after a few minutes' thought, stands on her little stool to see what can be seen out of the window. Trees in the square, chimneys and roofs. When she opens the window, the constant background hum, the clip-clop, the shouts, bangs, and crashes of a city. How to escape? That's what prisoners do, isn't it? She leans out as far as she can – not very far, since the windowsill is almost at the level of her shoulders. The roof stretches out to both sides. Perhaps she might be able to climb out and reach the ground through another house. But then, it's a long way to the ground. If she should fall, that would most probably be the end of her. But she made more adventurous climbs when she was younger. And she didn't fall then, so why should she not succeed here, too? She closes the window, happier now.

Time passes. People are adjustable. That's how the little, defenceless, forked animals that we are survive in a world filled with predators and hostile environments – ice, desert, rock, salt water. If you were to take a polar bear from its cold and icy playground to the nicely warm and dry desert, it will unfortunately not be grateful. It will die while the lizards who make the place their home dance in confused wonder around its furry feet. Take one of those lizards from its sun-basking rocky paradise to the kingdom of the ice-bear, and it will freeze to death in much the same time as it would in the freezer in your kitchen. But man and woman live full and happy lives (as far as that is possible in our world of sorrows) with both bear and lizard as neighbours. And so Jane adapts to her new life as half-prisoner in her grandmother's house.

For much of the time she is left alone. After a few days of timidity, she becomes bold enough to explore the entire house for herself. She finds a room full of books, which, although clean and tidy and smelling of beeswax, feels as if nobody has visited with greater intent than to dust and polish for quite some time. She meets the servants – there are four, since her grandmother needs to keep up a certain level of respectability, but is too tight-pursed to lay out more than is absolutely necessary. There's Mistress Garlic, the Cook (a woman whose name is an endless source of merriment to her friends, largely because she would no more eat garlic than suck on a piece of coal); Mr. Poker, the Butler; Daisy Sweetly, the maid of all work; and Jimmy Pocket, who is there for everyone else to look down on, in default of a cat to kick. They're not sure what to make of Jane and try not to commit themselves as they watch to see how the relationship between Jane and her grandmother develops.

Her grandmother takes an intermittent and unpredictable interest in her. Once she happens to be passing through the entrance hall as Poker opens the door to a visitor – a tall, dark man with a forbidding appearance. The man is shown into the study when her grandmother catches sight of Jane and introduces her to the man. "You know my granddaughter, Jane, of course." The man nods, "Of course." He turns to Jane. "Hardfist. Attorney at law," clearly not wishing to waste too many precious and valuable words on anyone who cannot be billed. The door closes behind him.

But at least once a day her grandmother is all smiles and welcome, determined to make her granddaughter enjoy her new life in London.

"New life?"

"Now that you live here, Jane."

"And, how long am I to live here, Grandmother?"

The question makes the old woman uncomfortable. "How long do young ladies live in their homes?" she says. Jane is silent. What can she mean? "Until they …"

"Yes?" prompts her grandmother.

"Until they marry?" Her grandmother nods slowly – this appears to be the right answer. But it terrifies Jane. "Or until they find something else …" she quickly, desperately adds. Her grandmother's eyebrows rise one at a time. "Something else?" she says. "What else can there be for a young … lady?"

Jane is unwilling to let this go. "Why, many things," she says, trying to appear calm while her mind desperately tries to think of one. Luckily her grandmother does not require a suggestion. She stands with a swish of skirts and glides noisily from the room. Turning in the doorway she announces (a little unnecessarily). "I have no desire for further discussion."

Jane watches the door close and feels … nothing. She cannot understand why her grandmother should want her here – why she should have gone to the effort to kidnap her, for that is what it was. There must be a reason. Or was it the General? Did he so much want to be rid of her that he arranged for her to be kidnapped and transported to London? The thought almost makes her sob, as she realizes how fond she has become of the strange, blustery old man in the few days that she was with him. For the rest of the day, she doesn't know what to do or feel. She hides in her little room on the top floor and watches the sun move across the wall. And as the daylight fades, she decides, "I cannot stay here. I cannot be a puppet. I shall do something."

ROOFTOPS

She can't sleep, so she has no difficulty in waiting until the house is still. She hears the last demanding ringing of her grandmother's bell; the last raking of embers in the grate; the final quiet creaks as Daisy Sweetly comes sweetly up the stairs to her little room. Daisy is the last in the house to be abed, and the first up in the morning, to make the fires and boil the water for washing. If she is lucky, she will have six hours of her own time every day, which riches she will fritter away in sleep. She and thousands like her are the lucky ones. They have somewhere to sleep and something to eat, and so they put up with a life of near slavery because the alternative is but the thickness of a door away and much, much worse.

At last Jane hears the creaking of Daisy's bed fall silent. Softly, she rises and tiptoes to the window, which she opened long ago to save any danger of noise in the night. She has already moved the chair to stand ready, so all she has to do now is to climb carefully onto the chair and gently and quietly pull herself up and through the window, so that she is lying on the roof, behind the parapet which runs along the front of the house.

She is breathless with excitement, though not fear. She has no fear of heights. And she has no fear of whatever she might find in the world she is about to enter, since the thought of staying with her grandmother is much worse, and leaves her feeling completely stifled. She feels excitement and happiness that she is at last doing something for herself.

Clouds partly cover the sky, but when it appears the moon is bright. Which is just as well, because street lighting is rare in the capital and dim candle-light does little to ease the darkness of the streets outside a house, where people find their way around after dark by hiring people with lanterns to show them the way.

She crawls along the roof, looking around as her eyes become accustomed to the darkness. She slowly relaxes as she begins to get an idea of the geography of the rooftops. Grand town houses though they are, they are nevertheless not separate buildings, so she can cover the whole side of Cavendish Square by scampering – carefully – along the roof from one house to the next. Reaching the end, she follows the line of the roof around the street corner. Freedom makes her feel light and airy, and she laughs aloud with happiness. But still she is neither cat nor bird, and at this moment can't see a way of getting down to the street without hurting herself, and without being seen by the watchman. She has reached another corner. What's the use in going round and round? She begins to feel that she'll have to face up to it. Getting out to the roof is not the same as being on the ground.

The wind, which she hasn't noticed before, grows stronger and makes her shiver. Her excitement and happiness have drained away and she's cold and miserable. But there's still hope. Above her the same wind is pushing the clouds ahead of it and over the sea to France, uncovering the moon for longer periods to cast its light on the garden below her. She sees a tree and her heart lifts. But the tree is too far from the roof to be of any help. She sees a bird's nest resting against the inside of the parapet above the garden. And she sees a spindly branch rising above the edge of the roof. She's excited again and scampers eagerly to the corner overlooking the garden. A climbing plant of some sort seems to cover the whole of the wall of the house. And its branches are thick and anchored firmly to the brick. She wonders if she dares try to climb down it. What if her weight pulls it away from the wall? What if she slips and falls? What if the watchman comes by just as she is hanging in mid-climb? All good reasons not to try. But she doesn't hesitate long. The only alternative would be to sneak back to her little attic room and her grandmother; and if she did that, she wouldn't be able to look herself in the eye again. She'd be too ashamed. So she rolls over on her tummy and feels for the branches with her feet, gripping as hard as she can with her hands as she begins the slow and terrifying fifty-foot journey down.

She feels worn out by the time she reaches the ground. She wants to collapse on the cool grass and sleep. But of course she can't. And she begins to laugh. What an idiot! She's let herself with great danger into – a walled garden. There must be a gate. There must be a way in from the street. Surely not everyone comes in through the front door. She's right. There is a gate – hidden behind a tree. She pulls gratefully at the handle. Locked. Her spirits fall again. She looks up. A branch of the tree reaches out over the wall. That's better! More climbing. She's very glad of all those times during her childhood in India when she refused to do what people told her, but instead ran wild with her friends, the local children. The climb is easier than she expected. There must be children in the house, because there is a treehouse in the tree, with a ladder helpfully fixed to the trunk. Two minutes later she is hanging by her arms over the street. She lets go, and lands softly without even falling over.

"Stop there, girl. Stop exactly where you are!"

In panic, she hears the running feet of more than one watchman.

THE GENERAL RIDES

The General is not a happy man, and everyone has noticed. He has been wrestling with his conscience ever since he allowed Jane to be taken away. It's true that he knew nothing about young girls, and was even less interested. It's true that his life revolves entirely around his friends, horses, gambling, and drinking – all in moderation, of course. Compared to a great many others of his acquaintance.

"She was here only a little while," he said to himself. "I enjoyed meself before, and I can enjoy meself just as well now. It's all back to normal. That's good. Nothing has changed." So he tries to persuade himself. But it's not true that nothing has changed. He has grown fond of the little thing, and he has done wrong by her. And being an upright and honourable man and a soldier … well, his life has turned uncomfortable now. Lumpy.

The General sits in his drawing room staring out of the window. He feels restless, but he can't settle to anything. He tries reading, but he realizes his eyes have reached the bottom of a page and he has no idea of what the page contained. He never has been a great reader. He throws down the book and takes up a pack of cards, but they carry no charms for him. He decides to go for a walk and is halfway to the gate when he is drained of the desire to go any further. He is turning back to the house when James rides up beside him.

"You're not yourself, General. It's vexing. What are we going to do about it?"

"That's it! We must do something."

James leads him to the familiar corner of the inn and furnishes him with a consoling cup of wine.

"I did wrong. I caved in. Me an old soldier, and I collapse like a badly-erected tent at the first sign of a breeze."

"Anyone would have done the same, old man."

"They wouldn't, you know. They would have stood up to the villain, just as I should have done. If it hadn't been for the business of the Lady and the Burgundy ... How did they know?"

James takes another long draught of wine. "Seems to me there's only two ways you can go ..." He waits for the General to ask him to reveal his wisdom. The General is staring into the bottom of his mug. He hasn't heard a word. "General!"

"What? Yes. Absolutely right. I agree. You're right, my friend. You always are."

James claps him around the shoulder. A rare thing to do, but James is feeling particularly sorry for his friend. "General, either you make up your mind that she's gone and forget about her ..."

"Or?" the General blinks hopefully at his friend.

"Or you go and get her."

It does the trick. The craggy and brittle General softens and relaxes. His shoulders ease and straighten. He sits up and takes a long sup at his wine. He turns to James with the first smile that has creased his cheeks for some time.

"Yes," he says. "That's it."

The next morning brings a new and cheerful light to shine across the countryside and in through the windows of Nightride Priory. It's wasted on the General, since he is a little the worse for wear, and oblivious to the world. The cheerful sun is beginning to look forward to its afternoon nap by the time the General's eyes spring slowly open. So great has been his relief at coming to the end of his depression that he and James have celebrated rather longer than they should. But, in spite of his sore head, he is still cheerful soon after noon when Darkling respectfully suggests it might be time to rise.

"We'll win this campaign, Darkling!" he announces.

"Certainly, General." Darkling usually doesn't trouble to ask what the General is talking about.

"Get Thunderfoot saddled. James and I are off to London!"

"Riding all the way, sir?" At last Darkling is surprised.

"Riding? Of course. Can't campaign in a coach. What do you take me for?"

"Very well, General." Darkling whispers from the room.

The General is so eager to be on his way that he almost knocks James off his horse as he canters through the gates of

Nightride Priory on his trusty Thunderfoot. James is always ready to tag along on an adventure, and he's a cheerful man, generally speaking, but he isn't as full of enthusiasm as the General when he's decided on something. So he approaches sedately on his somewhat elderly mare as the General comes charging forth from the gates of his house.

"Woah, Thunderfoot!" cries the General, seeing his friend too late …

"An apt name for the beast," says James, drily.

"Come on. No time to waste …"

And so their journey begins: the fat General on his fat horse, with his lanky friend on his skinny mare. As their outline darkens into silhouette, to the small children playing in the stream by the ford they look a bit like the cartoon by Mr. Hogarth that hangs on their schoolroom wall.

The weather is good. There's been no rain for some days, so the road is almost free from mud and water. But there are still several carts with broken wheels, or wedged axle-deep in puddles that looked shallow but turned out not to be.

"We were right to ride and not take the coach," says James.

They ride through the green hills of Wiltshire, passing with great care through the deep, dark, and ancient Savernake Forest, looking warily around for robbers all the while. They breathe more easily as they emerge on the other side, not realizing themselves how they'd been holding their breath. All in all they make good time, and arrive at the Bear in Hungerford by mid-afternoon where they stop for refreshment.

"We'll be in London tomorrow," says James as they settle comfortably in the corner.

"Tonight, if I have my way," replies the General heartily. James decides that he's joking and says nothing. He takes a mouthful of bread and wine. Chewing thoughtfully, a little like a very thin cow, he says, "Do we know where she is?"

"Who?"

"The gel."

"Not for sure. But I have my ways. One thing I am sure of – not my sister, but her mother lies behind this. Somehow. Don't know how, but I shall find out in no time. Mark my words."

James is confused. "Is not your sister's mother also …"

"No, damn your eyes. Not at all. Same father. Different mothers. Nasty woman. You'll see …"

They set off again. The General constantly wants to race ahead, but James refuses to exhaust his lanky mare for what he privately feels is just another of the General's wild goose chases. At Newbury, James insists they stop for the night. "Plenty of room at the George and Pelican," he says. "Always is. And they've a theatre. Capital stuff."

"What do I want with a theatre?" The General can hardly contain his astonishment. But James is uncharacteristically firm. He wants a clear head in the morning and refuses to spend the next few hours drinking. And he's looking forward to seeing a show, something he hasn't done for a very long time.

So the General lets his friend have his way and they stop for the night at Newbury. They even visit the theatre in the evening – and there the General receives a mighty shock that he certainly hadn't expected. One that makes him feel even worse about himself, and even more determined to succeed in the campaign to retrieve his niece.

ACTORS

The General doesn't really want to go to the theatre, but he does it to please his friend. So naturally they're late and find when they reach the door that there are no seats left.

"Room in the gallery, gents. You see much more up there."

A smile breaks out on the General's face. He's thinking there's nothing for it but to return to the inn and make themselves comfortable for the evening. But James is not going to be disappointed and cheerfully pays for two gallery tickets for them.

The gallery is already full and the floor covered in pieces of nutshell and orange peel. It's hot and noisy and the little stage seems a long way away. The General becomes steadily more ill-tempered – especially since his feet are already beginning to ache. But then the crowd becomes quieter as the musicians appear (all four of them) to blast out a rousing fanfare, followed by a rollicking jolly tune which has the audience swaying along. This overture tells the crowd to shut up and pay attention and draws them in to the opening of the story. The curtains part. The music becomes mournful. The tale begins.

It's a melodrama. There's lots of sighing and swooning (of ladies), lots of brandishing of guns and evil leering (of men), all generously larded with an amount of gesturing and declaiming (from everyone).

The story concerns a young woman who is being forced into marriage by her grandparents, who desperately want to be connected to the aristocracy. She, of course, loves her childhood friend, a poor farm lad. The crowd is undemanding and oohs, aahs, gasps, and laughs at all the right moments. James has a constant broad grin on his face, he's enjoying himself so much. The General follows the story with mild interest – until there comes a moment when suddenly he stands on tiptoe, the better to see, and cries out, "Good God. It's him! The devil. Damn him, the devil …"

On the stage strides a young man dressed all in black and bearing a pistol in each hand. He is come to seduce the young lady heroine – another obstacle and temptation to endanger her happiness. "Blackguard!" shouts the General, and the audience join in by hissing and booing the evil character. But that isn't the General's meaning. He grabs James by the arm and pulls him from the gallery, down the stairs and out. "What is it, old friend?" James is actually quite worried.

"That young devil on the stage, doncher see?"

"What? Don't I see what?"

"That was the villain who talked about the er … Lady and the er …"

"You mean, he …?"

"And took young Jane away."

James is amazed. But the General is angry. "That I should have been taken by … by an … by an actor!" he explodes with equal contempt for the acting profession and for himself. "We'll have him. We'll have him, I say. And he will bring us to my niece."

They will wait in the shadows for the actors to come out after the show – James has to explain the stage door to his friend. They will surprise the villain and force him to take them to the girl. An actor is no match for an experienced and valorous soldier. Their troubles are over.

So they believe.

WATCHMEN

But leave the General and his companion shivering in the midnight chill – nothing will happen for a little while, and you'll gain nothing by watching them stamp their feet, and peer repeatedly at their timepieces. While they are so fruitfully occupied, return with me – yes, we've been here before – to a place perhaps sixty miles to the east of that stage door. Today, you travel with me in no more than the time it takes to say so. If only everything were as easy as words. Tomorrow, the General will need the whole day to make this journey – and it will require great effort. In thirty-five years' time the railway will be built and it will become possible to cover the distance in no more than two hours – although there will be a great deal of concern that the human body is unable to withstand the strains of travelling at so great a velocity as thirty miles an hour. But by then the General and James will be unable to experience this new wonder, resting as they will in the ground under their parish church.

So, at around the same time, and sixty miles to the east, here we are. On the corner of Cavendish Square in the night. A girl runs from a side-street and across the square, disappearing from our sight towards Oxford Street. She is followed by two heavy men in watchmen's livery, bearing staves and panting heavily. They are not as fit as they used to be and she is powered by fear. It's not long before they give up and stand wheezily shaking their heads in shame and disappointment.

"She'll finish up in Newgate one way or another," they console each other and turn to stroll gently along the northern side of the square. And you will see that they are very nearly right.

Jane has crossed Oxford Street and dives into the smallest alley she could find. She's now far into Soho, blundering along the dark streets, looking for she knows not what. Somehow she finds her way to the centre of the labyrinth and, not knowing what else to do, settles against a tree on the grass of Soho Square to wait for daylight and an idea of what to do next.

But her night isn't over yet. She watches curiously as a figure bearing a lantern approaches from Greek Street. She cuddles tighter to the tree, hoping to merge her shadow with the trunk. Which would have worked, had the lantern-bearer not been accompanied by a curious and friendly dog. Its cold nose on her neck makes Jane giggle. She strokes the dog's fur, receiving a long, warm, wet slurp across her face as a reward. And then the dog's owner catches up with it, a terrifyingly large shadow towering over her. She shrinks back against the tree, as if hoping that she might make herself disappear like a ladybird into the folds of the bark. The man holds his lantern out towards her, the better to see what he has on the ground before him.

"A strange time and place for a little girl," he murmurs. Something about the lilt of his voice sparks memories in Jane. The lamp is now between them, so she can see very little of the man, but she can see his legs, and his waist, and hanging from his waist, a kirpan. She feels a flood of hope at the sight of the familiar curved knife.

"Kithede o?" she says. "Punjab?"

The man takes a startled pace backward; squats down to have a closer look at her.

"Who are you?" he asks – also in Punjabi.

"Suri," says Jane. She scrambles to her feet, warily taking a step away from the man. "You are Sikh ... your kirpan ..."

"And how is it that at the darkest time of night in the darkest of places in the deepest part of the city I find a little English girl who speaks to me in Punjabi and knows the Sikh kirpan?"

"Who can know the reason?" says Jane, with a little smile.

"You should be home in your bed."

"I have no home."

The Sikh holds the lantern closer to her face, looking at her closely.

"If you are not frightened of me, then I will not be frightened of you. You can come to my home and tell me how it is you are here."

That little voice in her head tells Jane that whatever she decides now will change her life for ever. But where else can she go? She nods. "Thank you," she says.

CONFUSE HER ENEMIES

By now, the General and James are nicely frozen and completely bored. They have watched the audience stream through the theatre courtyard, making their way to their nice, welcoming home fires or to the mulled wine of the inn. They have waited as the traffic on the street outside thins and falls silent. Finally, their waiting is rewarded. The stage door slams open and the actors and musicians pour forth in one rowdy group, talking and laughing all at the same time. Stiffly, the General forces himself forward, seeking out the young man they have been waiting for – and luckily for him, the young man is one of the last in the group. The General strides briskly up behind him, grabs him by the shoulder, and twists him around.

"Sir. I think we have matters to discuss!" says he. Confusingly, the young man shows no recognition in his face, and total calmness in the face of this assault.

"Do I know you, sir?" he asks languidly.

"I think you do, sir!" barks the General. "You were in my house, sir. And threatened me, sir. I wish to know the whereabouts of my niece."

The actor calmly takes a step back, looks around at his friends (who are all watching, fascinated) as if to say *we have a right one here*. A musician giggles, but is silenced by the General's furious look. "I know nothing of your niece; and nothing of you," says the actor. "Sir." And smirks again for the benefit of his companions.

"I think you do, sir."

"You call me a liar?"

The General opens his mouth, but the actor is quicker. "Have a care what you say, sir." The crowd of actors watches with amusement and nods of approbation at this cleverness. The General is reduced to spluttering. "Will you call me out, sir? An actor! Pah!"

The actor remains calm and low-voiced. "I think you'll find I'm as good a man in a duel as you, old man."

At this point James steps in. "Come, General, the man says he doesn't know you. Perhaps you are mistaken."

Without waiting for the General's reaction, the young actor nods, turns away, and with outstretched arms drives his companions before him towards their waiting refreshment. The General is left shaking with cold, anger, and frustration.

"This is the wrong man, General," says James, soothingly.

"He's an actor, dammit. He can act. How can you know if what he says is true? His profession is to appear that which he is not."

But for all his anger and frustration, the General has no alternative but to allow James to lead him away. Calling the potboy to stoke up the fire in the nearly deserted room, James orders a jug of mulled wine to warm them both, and soon, as the warmth spreads within and without, they become a little more cheerful.

So we'll leave them there by the fire, where James succeeds in persuading the General that he must have been mistaken after all, and we'll take a few steps outside into the refreshing air of the night.

Do you hear that? Look, over there, across the yard. A stable door is opening slowly, though all is dark inside. In the fitful moonlight, as clouds move across the sky, can you see the man leading a black horse from the stall? Now he mounts and walks his horse across the yard. He looks down and catches sight of you. You're sure it's the young actor, but his face is angry at the sight of you, and he seems to snarl. He spurs his mount. Horse and man leap out of the yard and away down the road to London. They're going fast – you hear the pounding of hooves in the quiet night for quite some minutes.

JANE KNOWN AS SURI

In a small house in Dean Street, Jane is sleeping now. Her new Sikh friend has brought her to his home, where he lives alone but for two servants. He has given her hot chai, and a pillow for her head, and a blanket to keep her warm. They have not spoken much. Without words, they have saved talk for the morning, and Jane is very tired.

The house smells of the spices of home, and when she sits down to samosas and chai in the morning she bursts into tears. Her host looks worried. "How have I upset you?" he asks, and the childlike expression of worry on the face of such a big bearded warrior of a man makes her laugh.

"You haven't upset me," she says. "All this ... it's just like ... I miss my home so much."

Without thinking, she pours out her whole story to her new friend – her childhood, her mother, her father's murder; that she feels so alone in England, with no friend and no home. He listens and nods and smiles.

"You poor, lost child," he says. "What will you do now?"

Jane has no plan other than to escape the clutches of her Grandmother, and the prison in Cavendish Square.

"You may stay a little while …" A wide smile breaks out on Jane's face, and she palpably restrains herself from running across the room to hug him. He raises his hand as if to slow her down, "… a day or two, not more. Soon you will have to leave here." He pauses, considering how much to say, and falls silent. Jane is too happy and relieved to notice. "Thank you," she says.

Lak (that's his name) trusts her well enough to leave her alone in the house when he goes out soon afterwards. (Alone, that is, except for the maid.) She is very quickly bored. The house is not large, and once she has spent ten minutes exploring it, she finds herself sitting at an upstairs window, staring out at the street, people-watching.

And it's lucky for her that she's there. She sees a man approach the house, tall, dark, and severe. She knows she's seen him before but can't remember where.

Just as he's about to knock at the door, Lak comes back. It's clear the two men know each other, and they talk rapidly and in low voices outside the front door. Jane looks down with curiosity and growing suspicion. Something feels wrong. And with a gasp she remembers. The man is Hardfist. Her grandmother's lawyer. Why is he here? She runs from the window in terror. Lak has betrayed her. Desperately she runs to the back of the house. But there's nothing but a tiny yard and a high wall out there. She runs up the narrow stairs to the servants' rooms in the attic. Perhaps she can climb on to the roof again. But the doors are locked. She hears a voice from below, and the heavy tread of someone coming wearily up the stairs.

"Excuse me, miss. Is there anything you're wanting?" The maidservant appears around the corner of the stairs. There's no way out. She's trapped.

Meanwhile our young actor has arrived in London and is at this moment giving his sweating horse over to the care of the stables of the Golden Cross Inn at Charing Cross where he takes a room for a night, paying in advance with the last coin he possesses, but confident that the news he carries will provide him with more. It's a few minutes' walk to Hardfist's chambers, but it will be quicker to go on foot than to take a horse through the crowds on the Strand and the alleys towards the Inns of Court.

He strides past the theatre in Drury Lane, turning his head to consider – just for a moment – what it would be like to perform on that stage. He dances around the angry flower-seller that he so nearly walked into, and catches sight of Hardfist on the corner ahead.

Hardfist, you will remember, is on his way back from Soho and his brief meeting with Lak. He is not pleased to see the young actor.

"What is it? I told you to stay away from London."

"Sir … I thought you might like to know, sir. The General is on his way."

"Why would it interest me what the old fool decides to do?"

"I imagine he is looking for his niece."

"Of course he's looking for his niece.

But he doesn't know where she is, and how is he to find her in a city as big as London?"

The actor has no answer. He can feel his chances of dinner melting away. "I thought …" he says, struggling to think of something persuasive to say. Hardfist reaches into his pocket and gives him a sixpenny piece. "You took trouble. I know that. Now go." He waves away any thanks that might be coming and walks on. But he is now deep in thought, and at the street corner he turns so as to go back the way he came, in the direction of Cavendish Square.

And the young actor looks with despair and a certain amount of anger at the sixpence in his hand. At least he will be able to eat tonight, he thinks; but he has no other money. Perhaps he might become in reality the highwayman he has been playing on the stage. After all, he still has his horse. He'll do anything to stay out of the slums where Hardfist last found him. Anything at all. He begins to think that he might be able to get some money from the General. Perhaps it's time to change sides.

Lak comes into the house and finds Jane standing waiting for him. She looks as if she has been crying. "What's the matter, Suri?" he says, with dismay.

"Who was the man outside?"

"What man?"

"You were talking at the front door. I was upstairs at the window."

For just a second, Lak looks alarmed – which is not reassuring to Jane. "What did you hear that worried you?" he asks, not sounding quite as sympathetic as he intended to.

"I heard nothing. Who is he?"

"He comes from the landlord – the owner of this house. We talked about the rent that I pay him, and he asked if I knew any other people who need a house to rent. Nothing to worry you, Suri. Why do you ask?"

"Because he's my grandmother's lawyer. I thought … I thought …"

Lak smiles. "I didn't know, Suri, so I could not betray you to him. You have no need to fear. And in any case," he adds, "how could I betray you, a countryman of my own, when I am here in this city so that I can help my country?"

"There are no British in the Punjab," says Suri. "Only a few like me."

"No." Suddenly Lak is very serious. "But more will come, and we must fight them. And the best way to fight is to know your enemy and the way he thinks; so you know what he will do. I am here to watch and learn so that I will understand my enemy."

She spends the rest of the day feeling that she is two people. Suri is happy that her home will be defended; but Jane, although she has been in Britain only a little while, feels it's somehow wrong to know this freedom fighter, and to say nothing. But who could she speak to? And who would believe her, a young girl newly arrived from the other side of the world? The General would know what to do. Tomorrow, she decides, she will find her way out of London and start her journey back to Nightride Priory.

THE GENERAL WALKS

As Suri and Lak are talking, the General is leading an increasingly reluctant James towards the house in Cavendish Square.

They arrived in London late last night. Though they were both exhausted from the long ride, the General was all for riding right up to the front door in Cavendish Square. James persuaded him that it was more sensible to wait till morning, by the simple expedient of falling from his horse in the inn yard. He was so tired. He revived well enough to put away a large slice of pie and a bumper of wine before falling, already asleep, into bed.

And as the morning dawns, pausing only for the short time sufficient to take in a small breakfast of toasted bread, eggs, kedgeree, and devilled kidneys, the General strides out with James through the western streets of London towards the house where he is sure he will find his niece.

He would have been the first of several to arrive that morning, but he loses his way. He is not a natural Londoner. He has visited before – to receive military commissions and on family occasions – but his grasp of geography and his sense of direction are hazy at best. He and James repeatedly find themselves at Hyde Park.

So leave them to sort themselves out. While they walk in the wrong direction along Oxford Street, Hardfist is admitted to the house and waits impatiently in the drawing room on the first floor. At last, Jane's grandmother makes her entrance into the room. She has kept Hardfist waiting to remind him of her superior position – but also because she does not often rise early, and is rarely prepared to meet the world before noon.

"Madam," Hardfist comes close to bowing. She is not of the aristocracy, so does not merit a bow. On the other hand it's important to Hardfist to keep her happy, and a little flattery is always useful, even if his teeth are gritted together to keep in the things he really wants to say but dare not.

"What is so important that you disturb me so early, and unannounced?" she says with a brittle smile.

"I thought you might like to know,"

he pauses, hoping to take back a little control and have her ask what he is going to tell her; but she simply spreads her formal smile even more thinly and waits for him. "The General is on his way here. If he is not already in London, he will arrive very shortly."

"I see. And how is it that you are so intimate with the General?"

"Madam, I have my sources of information." And Hardfist at last allows himself a moment of superiority. Grandmother remains unimpressed.

"Hm. Very good. I shall await his arrival," she says. Hardfist is dismissed. She doesn't tell him that Jane is no longer here, and that she has no idea where the girl has gone. At least she will soon discover whether the General has her. Naturally she betrays none of this to Hardfist, who soon finds himself on the pavement, feeling sorry for himself. If only he were not so poor, he thinks, he would be able to choose the people he allows to treat him badly. Meanwhile there's the butcher's account to pay, and the rent. Already he has no home but his run-down chambers – those two damp rooms where he has to sleep, too, though this is possibly his greatest secret.

The General finds his way to the house just as Hardfist slinks sadly round the corner.

"Got 'im!" cries James happily, talking of the house. "Cornered at last!" Life is just one long hunt to James. The General's feet are hurting him. He doesn't answer and watches as James pulls on the doorbell. And soon they are waiting inside, exactly as Hardfist was made to wait.

"Jolly comfortable chairs, what?" James likes to find something positive in every situation. It's a skill he's become expert in, since, truth be told, his life has not generally been easy or comfortable. He would be shocked if you were to say that to him, since his ability to look on the bright side is so well-developed that he doesn't even notice it. Life is simply rosy for him.

The General is more of a realist and begins to pace impatiently up and down. He knows that Grandmother is playing a game of power, and deeply resents being its subject. At last! Here she is. He spins in his most military manner to face her.

"Good morning, George. Well, it has been quite a while, has it not?"

"Good day to you, Madam."

"And how can I be of assistance to you, dear George?"

"You have my niece," the General barks.

"What of it?"

"Her father sent her to me. I've come to take her back."

The lady smiles, calm as a summer day. "I'm afraid that won't be possible." Naturally, the General doesn't believe her. "Madam, I will go through this house from top to bottom …"

"From attic to cellar …" James chimes in, standing in support of his friend.

"If that's what I have to do," continues the General. "But, Madam, I will leave with my niece in my care."

"She's not here," the lady has a delicate air of triumph about her, and takes a theatrical few moments to enjoy the surprise on the faces of her visitors. "She's with my lawyer," she continues. "You might have seen him, he left only a few minutes before you arrived." She pauses again, and her voice hardens, just the teensiest bit. "As you know, gentlemen," she says, "and as my lawyer will confirm, possession is nine points of the law. Good day, gentlemen. I wish you a comfortable journey back to Wiltshire." She glides out of the room, calling instructions to Poker (her butler) to show the gentlemen out. (Poker is already standing next to her in the doorway, since he has been listening and watching through the keyhole, but it's important to keep up appearances, and he is accustomed to having instructions shouted at close range.)

The General is of course perplexed and disappointed. But you and I have the advantage of him. We know that Jane is not with Hardfist – but we know no better than the General what she will do now.

TO FAVOUR CURRY

She is resolved. She will leave London now – somehow – and find her way back to the General. She comes down from the bedroom looking for Lak in the drawing room on the first floor. He has a visitor – another Sikh, who looks surprised to see her. "Dhanbaad," she says, "Thank you. I'll go now. I hope we meet again – maybe in India."

Lak seems surprised. "Not yet," he says. "We would like to talk to you. Please come in."

They tell her to leave the door open, so that she knows she can leave any time. They don't want her to feel trapped. They ask her about her life, and whether she belongs in India, or here in England with her greater family. "India," she says, without a second's hesitation. They laugh at her enthusiasm and tell her that they are working to keep India free – to prevent yet another invader from ruling the whole sub-continent. They say they are putting a great trust in her now, because already she knows enough to endanger their lives. They pause and look at each other. This is the big question. "Will you help us?"

She's surprised more than anything else. "How can I help you? I don't know anything." They laugh. "You speak Punjabi. You speak English. And both you speak as a native. There are people here who will find this very useful."

"So do you. There must be lots of people who speak lots of languages."

They smile. "But you are unique because you are English," Lak says. "We know of a person who will be very glad indeed of your help, and he will trust you because you are a young English girl and know nothing."

"What do you want me to do?"

"We would like you to help him in his translations."

"And then?"

"And then we would like you to come to us and tell what you have seen."

Suri is still not sure she understands. "Who is this person?" she asks.

"He is an English Colonel."

She feels a thrill of excitement, and she shivers. "You want me to be a spy?" she says. In unison they waggle their heads, yes. Their teeth beam smiles at her. She looks around, not knowing what to do. A spy. They wait patiently for her answer. "How will I find this colonel?" she asks.

The Hindoostani Coffee House near Portman Square offers the best of food and hospitality from the sub-continent of India. Cooking, service, and décor are lavish, and the house is popular both with people like Lak, and with the many British people who are involved with India. (Unfortunately, popular though it is, the place is expensive to run on such a scale, and is losing money. Later this year Dean Mahomet, the owner, will be declared bankrupt. But that is yet to come.) A regular visitor to the coffee house, Colonel Jenkins, has asked Dean Mahomet if he knows of a trustworthy person who can help with translations from Punjabi; and so the request has found its way to Lak, who that evening brings Jane to the restaurant and gives her into the care of the owner himself. She nervously says goodbye to Lak and follows Dean upstairs to a withdrawing room, where she finds two Englishmen talking quietly while enjoying smoking a hookah. They look up briefly, "Evenin', Mahomet," one of them grunts, and they return to their conversation. "I have your translator, Colonel," says Dean.

"Where is he?"

"She is here," and Dean pushes Jane further into the room.

"This? Thought her a servant. Are you making fun of me, Mahomet?"

"No, sir. She is fluent in English and in Punjabi, having grown up in the Punjab; is that not right, girl?" Jane nods.

"Can you read, girl?" asks the Colonel. She nods again.

"You know, Colonel," says his companion, languidly, "might be just what we need if she's any good. Harmless little girl. Knows nothing. Less of a risk than some of these other fellows here. Never know who their friends are."

The Colonel nods slowly. "Come here, girl. What's your name?"

"Jane, sir."

"Read this, Jane." He pulls a folded piece of paper from a pocket. It's a letter. She reads.

"No, damn you for a little fool. In

English. Why do you think you're here?"

Jane translates, "From Lahore in haste, greetings. I have heard only today that their commanders will gather in Delhi on the tenth day of next month. If you wish I will meet you with more information. In case this messenger is not to be trusted, you will be told on what day and in which place."

The Colonel's companion laughs and slaps his knee in delight, "'In case this messenger cannot be trusted …' He was right, too, damn him for a suspicious clever devil."

The Colonel reaches out and takes the letter from Jane's hand. "Very good," he says. "Of course, this is old news. I wonder if you can be so useful when it really matters."

"I can only do my best, sir," Jane says. The Colonel smiles. "Yes, that's all that any of us can say. And who are you, girl? Where do you come from? How are you here?"

"Why should we trust you?" adds his companion. So Jane tells a short version of her life so far – a girl growing up far from her people, isolated in a part of the sub-continent the British had not yet reached. Her father had given her such a longing for England, she says, that when he died, she couldn't wait to travel at last to her ancestral home. There's a silence as she finishes. Both men are looking at her appraisingly. "Sounds perfect, eh, Colonel?"

"Or too good to be true," says the Colonel. He sighs, "But it does no good to look a gift horse, isn't that right?" He stands. "Come with us, my girl. We have some more recent letters for you to look at."

Jane is a little nervous at this, wondering where they might want to take her; but she realizes she has no choice if she is to help Lak as she has promised. She follows the two soldiers down the stairs and through the dining room.

"George! By George," cries the Colonel's companion. (We really must begin referring to him by his name, which is Cecil. His rank is Major, and he's a little like a military version of the General's friend James, except with more money at his disposal. A lot more money. That, in fact, is how he came to the rank of Major, by buying it. Everyone does it. The Army's explanation is that this avoids favouritism and promotes impartiality, and the system will continue for another sixty glorious years.)

"Cecil!" cries the General, who is at a table with James, napkin around his neck, tucking into a plate of curry. "And Jane, my dear …" The General stands, pulling the tablecloth with him. James hastily grabs at it to prevent its fall to the floor, glasses, plates and all – while the General and Jane embrace in a way they never would have done before. The Colonel turns to Cecil, "I think we can put our doubts to bed, eh Major?"

"The General is my dearest friend," says Cecil. "Saved me from meself many a time."

Luckily for Jane, in the enthusiasm and confusion of the greetings, nobody asks her to explain how she came to be in the Hindoostani Coffee House that evening.

And what are the General and James doing there? It's nothing but a coincidence. Seeing his friend look so downhearted as they emerged from the house in Cavendish Square, James remembered hearing of this Indian restaurant which wasn't far away, and persuaded his friend to cheer themselves up a little by going there in the evening, rather than riding straight back to Wiltshire.

And before we continue, let me tell you of one or two other things of interest that have occurred in Cavendish Square this day.

He feels undignified, but he already knows there is no dignity in poverty, so he waits, hidden amongst the bushes in the gardens at the centre of the Square. It's our friend the actor – Robert – watching the door of the house and thinking of ways in which he can mitigate the emptiness of his purse. The door opens. As the door begins to open, Robert straightens himself and begins to walk so that he will pass the house as if hurrying to some weighty meeting. Just as he'd hoped, the General and James step onto the pavement. James sees the actor first and tries to turn his friend away. But it's too late. "You again!" roars the General. "Be gone before I have you sent to Newgate for the thief and kidnapper that you are."

Robert draws deeply on his acting ability and does not run, as would be his instinct. "General," he says, as smoothly as he can manage. "I have come to see the error of my ways. I regret what I did, and should like to be of assistance to you. Perhaps I can undo some of the damage that I have done." The General looks at him suspiciously. Behind his back, James waves his arms around encouragingly, as if to say, *go on, then, speak.*

"I take it you have not found your niece, and I think I may be able to help, sir …"

If anyone ever really did harrumph, it would be the General at this point. "And I imagine you want money for this?"

Robert clears his throat and looks at the General's shoes. "Well, sir, I am not a rich man …" he says.

"Oh, give him a coin or two," says soft-hearted James, and – though he splutters – the General rummages in his purse. "What do you give us in return?" he says as he hands over the coins.

"I confess I cannot say *exactly* where she is at this very moment. But," he continues quickly before the General can object. "I know who will have her, and I can bring her to you."

Reluctantly they agree that he will seek them out at their lodgings the next morning – another reason why they delay their return to Wiltshire.

But our actor does not leave the Square as they do. He returns to his hiding place in the bushes – now with a happy smile on his face, jingling coins in his hand, and the certainty of a full stomach for a few days at least. And he waits for the door to open again.

He does not have to wait long. Grandmother clips sharply on the pavement, calling out to Poker to find her a cab – even though one is turning the corner at this very moment. Once again Robert takes his courage in both hands and approaches the Lady. She ignores him, at first, behaving exactly as if he were not standing two feet away from her.

"Excuse me, Madam," he speaks firmly but respectfully.

"Who are you?"

"Nothing but a poor actor, Madam – but I am an agent of Mr. Hardfist, and it was I who brought your granddaughter from the country."

"You want money?"

"I believe you are unsure of her whereabouts – and I know, too, that the General is in London."

"I really have not the slightest notion of what you mean, young man."

"Madam, I believe I can return your granddaughter to you."

She pauses. "And no doubt you would expect a reward?"

"Great People know how to reward loyalty, Madam."

She laughs – merrily, if a little scornfully. "Poker! Give this man a few shillings to tide him over."

"Thank you, Madam," says Robert. "You will not be disappointed."

"Make sure of it," she says, drily climbing into the waiting cab. Robert the actor watches her go and is happy that his life has turned for the better again. Jane known as Suri is not the only person playing a double game.

NIGHT ROOMS

While you were occupied in catching up on earlier events, the Colonel has taken Jane, the General, and their two companions by cab to his house, where he also has his offices. Candles are found and lit for them – the house was dark and closed for the night – and the Colonel settles them in the shadows.

"What's this all about, my friend?" asks the General. The Colonel pauses. "Well, I suppose there's no harm in allowing you to see. After all, you're a British military man."

"Indeed I am."

"It's about the Punjab, d'you see? The Northwest of India. It's rich, and it's the western gateway to the sub-continent. We need to control it."

"Naturally."

"Unfortunately – for them," the Colonel continues. "Some of the locals don't quite see our point of view and are making it quite difficult for us to – how shall I put it – expand our area of influence. Of course, everything you see and hear tonight is a secret of the highest order, and any gossip could be punished extremely severely." He looks at their faces one by one. "Extremely severely. Now …"

He takes a locked box from a drawer of his writing desk. "Come here, girl," he says. "Tell me what you make of this." He lays a crumpled sheet of paper on the desk and smooths it down with his hands. "What's that?" Jane points at a dark shape spreading from one edge of the paper. The Colonel peers closer. "Spilt his ink, I should guess," he grunts. "Either that or his blood. Can you read it, girl?"

She struggles to read in the flickering candlelight. "There is danger to Ranjit Singh – he rules the Punjab." Jane has stopped reading to explain to the Colonel.

"I know who he is, dammit. Why do you think you're here? What else does he say?" Jane lifts the paper closer to the candle flame. "Careful, girl!" The Colonel is finding it difficult not to shout at her. "Don't burn the damn thing."

That's exactly what Jane is trying to do; but she mustn't make it too obvious. "I'm trying to see," she complains. "The writing is very faint."

"Read it."

"He – or she – says that they must meet, because it is too dangerous to write what he knows."

"I said read it, girl. I want every word."

She reads, "We have many enemies. This cannot be written. We must talk in our familiar place …"

"When, girl, when?"

"I say, she's trying to help, Colonel." The General protests at the Colonel's impatience.

"On the second day of the week, two hours after dawn when there will be many people."

"Which week?"

"That's all he says," Jane looked up at him. "There was a little more, but it's blotted out by his blood."

"Or ink, young Jane," James swiftly interjects.

"Or ink," Jane echoes, all the while gazing at the Colonel. He turns away.

"Not as useful as we'd hoped," he says. "But thank you."

"What next?"

"We must deliver the letter, discover where the familiar place is, and meet them there …"

"So the girl has done her duty well?" the General asks.

"Indeed she has," the Colonel smiles.

"Excellent. And tomorrow we return together to the country."

"I'd rather you didn't … just in case," says the Colonel. "I would be most grateful if you were able to remain in London for a little while longer. And I'm sure His Majesty will be pleased to assist with any expenses …"

"Since he doesn't know which way is up," the Major smirks.

"The Regent, then."

Jane is quite relieved at this. It means that she won't have to invent a reason to stay in London, so that she can see Lak again. The General would rather go straight home this minute, but he agrees in the end – for the sake of the nation.

The Colonel sends a servant to find a cab, and they drive back through the late streets to the White Bear in Piccadilly, where James and the General are staying, and where the constant bustle and noise of a coaching inn is a surprising contrast to the quiet of the streets at this late hour. In all this activity they don't notice the dark figure thickening the shadows around the entrance to the inn yard.

BETRAYALS

"Didn't sleep a wink. Not a solitary second. So much damn noise in these places." The General is not in the best of humours. His temper is worse because he now remembers how much he hates London life. Not only has he agreed to remain here, but he has no idea of what to do with the little girl – though he is truly glad to see her again.

Jane is happy this morning. She knows what she has to do, and the challenge of finding a way of doing it secretly makes it even more exciting – well, it would, wouldn't it? She sends James to find a street map of London and spreads it on the breakfast table, pushing aside plates, mugs, and serving dishes. She squeaks with pleasure when she discovers that Dean Street is only a few minutes' walk away – and can't stop herself blushing when she remembers that she is supposed to be acting in secret. She also discovers that they are not very far from Cavendish Square, and she feels a pang of fear. It's such a little way between freedom and captivity; between success and failure. She can only trust that there are so many people in London that to find just one young girl in the crowd would be almost impossible. "I'm going for a walk," she announces. The General and James are both horrified, but she won't be dissuaded, and she and James walk out arm in arm together.

The entrance to the yard of a coaching inn is always busy – people come and go, others just hang around hoping for entertainment, or money, or a sale of a posy from their basket. But one of these loiterers has been here all night. He's damp and stiff-limbed. The night has been the longest of his life, and, while it hasn't actually rained, for several hours a fine mist has slowly soaked through everything and left the streets shining and slippery. Jane and James walk past him and pay him no particular attention. He waits a few seconds before hobbling awkwardly after them, hiding in the crowds; trying to coerce his legs into doing what they're told.

He's not alone. Our man Robert the actor has risen bright and early and strolled from his lodging at Charing Cross to watch outside the White Bear until Jane or the General should come out. He knows nothing of what has happened the previous evening, but he has already inquired at the inn and knows that they are still there. As it happens, he is lucky and doesn't have to wait long. He notices, too, the stiff-limbed follower, bobbing up and down in the crowds behind them as they walk away westward towards Hyde Park.

Yes. It's the wrong direction. Jane cannot shake James from her arm. He has seen her lost once and seen the surprising effect her disappearance had on his friend. He isn't going to let that happen again, and has determined not to let the girl out of his sight. And so they walk the length of Piccadilly to the park at the edge of London, and stroll amongst the riders on horse and in carriage, and the peacocks, both human and bird, there to display their beauty to anyone who will pay attention. It's a site so colourful that it reminds Jane of India, and so she is both happy and sad. Sad she is, too, because she worries more and more that something terrible will happen to Lak if she doesn't find some way of warning him.

James notices nothing. He is much too captivated by the horses in the park to pay much attention to Jane (also, every now and again, by a pretty woman – though it has to be admitted that women are generally a mystery to James, and they frighten him).

Eventually, they return to the White Bear. James has had a splendid time and is ready to tell the General all about it over a cup of wine. As they enter the inn yard, Jane detaches herself from his arm.

"I have to go to my room," she says. James looks blank. She lowers her voice, "Female things," she says, confident that this will terrify him sufficiently to prevent any further questions. He nods mutely. She's free.

The inn's rooms are across the yard from the taproom, where James and the General will be drinking. Jane does go to her room, but only long enough to collect a shawl with which to cover her head and shoulders and shade her face. She walks along the yard, passing the tap-room door, which is closed. The yard goes all the way through from Piccadilly to Jermyn Street behind, and so she comes out on to Jermyn Street, cuts through to the Haymarket, and as fast as she can go without running, she heads in the direction of Dean Street. She doesn't notice the shadow weaving through the crowded street behind her. He is happy at last. The trip to Hyde Park was a nightmare for him – there was hardly anywhere he could hide, and it was just so boring. Also, he was terrified that he might be recognized, since he knew many of the officers in the Horse Guards barracks on the edge of the park. But now, at last, the young lady is doing something she shouldn't, and it makes him smile. And Robert? Now he knows that Jane is back with the General, it's clear he won't be earning any money from him for the time being. Still, he watches to see what they will do before setting off for Cavendish Square. He hasn't seen Jane leave the yard, and he is waiting outside for the General and James. He will be waiting some time, since at the moment they are enjoying doing what they do best and seem to care neither about Jane nor about the time.

"What if no one is at home?" Jane is

thinking as she reaches the end of Dean Street. "I should write a note." She stops at a stationer and pleads with him for pen and paper. He is suspicious. There's always a trick about children, he's thinking. They send one of them in first, and while you're distracted, another one is picking your pocket or stealing your goods. He's hard to convince. Eventually, though, she gets her way and writes the note in the shop. The stationer will remember that it was in no script that he'd ever seen before. It was very ... ornamental; and she wrote the wrong way round – from right to left. He was glad when she left his shop.

She arrives at Lak's front door. She is about to ring the bell; instead, she looks around, up and down the street, in case he might be coming home. A little way down the street, a man turns suddenly and walks the other way. Something is familiar about him. She can't say quite what, and she feels suddenly cold. But if she is to deliver her letter, there is nothing else she can do. And there's no time for anything else. She pulls vigorously at the bell, watching the man walk away –

and seeing him look back at her before turning away again. She is jiggling with fearful impatience. At last the door opens. It's the servant. "Give him this. Quickly. It's urgent. And tell him beware strangers on the street. I have to go." She thrusts the letter into the hands of the servant and walks rapidly back down Dean Street. Her heart thumps as she comes closer to the man, who she is now sure has been following her. He pretends to be watching something over her head. She stops only a couple of feet away from him and waits until he drops his gaze to look at her.

"Young lady?"

She is terrified; but she thinks that if she can delay him for a few minutes it will give Lak a little extra time. "I have the foolish idea that you are following me, sir," she says. "I know your face, yet I am a stranger to London."

"Why would I trail around London behind a child?" He turns his back and sets off up the street in the direction of Lak's house. She runs around in front of him.

"I won't be pushed aside so easily,

sir. I see you everywhere ... Please explain."

He becomes angry. "I've no time for this," he says. "Here ..." He presses a sixpence into her hand and is away. But seeing the shape of his head as he turns again, she remembers where she has seen him before. He was in the Colonel's house last night.

So in her haste to save Lak and warn him of the trap, she has instead betrayed him.

SURROUNDED

She doesn't know what to do now. Going back to Lak's house will only make matters worse. And she has already been away from the White Bear too long. Sadly and slowly, she drags her way back to Piccadilly.

But by the evening she feels a bit better, and she has dragged the General and James along with her to the Hindoostani Coffee House. She tells them – quite truthfully – that the food makes her feel at home. She loves the warmth and the light and the smells of familiar spices. And she loves the mix of people, Indians and Europeans, talking together in a way she has never seen before. And also, she hopes to get a message to Lak or his friends.

Her pleasure is spoiled halfway through the meal by the arrival of the Colonel and his companion. She wants to run and hide, but before she has time even to stand up, they are pulling chairs from the next table and sitting down with them.

"Good evening, General," says the Colonel. "Capital to find you here. You and your companions." He looks very hard at Jane. The General does not trouble himself to look pleased.

"How can I be of service, Colonel? Got more reading for the girl?"

"Not for the moment. But I would like a word with her ... with your permission?"

The General grunts his agreement.

"You see, young lady," the Colonel begins. "I have received disturbing reports, which force me to consider how far I am able to trust you ..."

"Have a care, sir!" the General is outraged. The Colonel smiles –like a fox, Jane thinks.

"I mean no disrespect, General. If I am right, the lady will understand my meaning, and will perhaps be able to answer accordingly. If I am wrong, the lady will know nothing, and no harm is done." He turns to Jane. And waits.

She attempts her most innocent expression – the one developed to get her out of trouble at home in India, and subsequently refined by watching the English ladies travelling to England on the boat.

"I'm sorry to disappoint you, Colonel," she says, in the most adult manner. "I am happy to read your papers for you, but I cannot think what else you might mean." She gathers her skirts and her courage. "Excuse me for a moment, please." And she makes her way through the room towards the kitchen.

The Colonel follows, and catches up with her in the kitchen doorway. He takes her arm. "Sir!" she says. He leans closer and whispers. "If you are thinking of doing anything unwise, know that I have troopers surrounding the house."

After that, events tumble on one another, tangle together so that later she cannot say for sure how it all happens. She remembers running into the kitchen and shouting that soldiers were outside. She thinks that Lak must already have been there, for the next thing she remembers is Lak grabbing her and holding her wrists tight behind her back. His kirpan is held against her neck.

"We are leaving now," says Lak. "If you follow, or if you shoot, the girl will die."

DARKNESS AND DEPARTURE

Jane is so shocked, feels so betrayed and disappointed, so frightened, that all she can think about is not letting herself cry. The Colonel hesitates – which Jane thinks is a good thing. "Tell your soldiers to stand aside," Lak barks, pulling Jane backwards to the street door. She is aware of the cold air of the night outside, and the rattle of muskets preparing to fire. "Colonel!" Lak shouts. The Colonel appears in the doorway. "Let them pass," he says wearily.

Lak grips Jane tightly by the wrist, drags her stumbling along with him into the darkness. They run. Soon they are across Oxford Street and into the narrow streets of Soho – and further, to the tangled alleys of Covent Garden. The Colonel's people will never catch them now, though they feel bright as quicksilver in the dark – as though everyone must know them for what they are. *And what is that?* Jane asks herself. She thought she had a new friend – somebody with whom she felt more comfortable than anyone else in this strange land. And then he holds a knife to her throat and carries her off to she knows not where. A sob surges inside her, and involuntarily she begins dragging her feet. "Where are we going?" she says. Lak stops, but she can't see his face. "Help me," he says. "Come with me. Protect me. Pretend you are my captive." She nods, but he cannot see. She feels his hand on her cheek, and she nods again.

They continue together through the dark city. She's surprised by how well Lak seems to know his way. Much later, through the stink of the street, she smells the sourness of water. The river. But by then she simply wants it to stop.

Later she wakes in a strange room. Somebody puts a cup of hot chai on the floor near where she lies. Sunlight smudges on filthy window glass and burns everything from the room but the brightest white and the deepest shade. She moves away from the light to find the room really quite crowded. Perhaps a dozen men – all from the Indian sub-continent – are talking rapidly and quietly. She can't understand them, though she knows from the sound and some of the words that it's a language of India. "Punjabi?" she croaks. In sudden silence all twelve faces snap towards her. After a few seconds of staring, as if their heads were connected by a cunning and invisible system of pulleys and levers, they all turn away together and continue their chatter. It's as if she weren't there.

They pay her no attention as she makes her way to the door. But when she pulls on the handle she finds the door stuck. One of the men has moved and sits leaning against it. Still, he pays her no attention, but continues chattering with his friends. She is imprisoned with twelve strange men whose language she doesn't understand.

The sun has moved until it no longer shines into the room; and, at last, the door opens. The man sitting on the floor doesn't move fast enough and is pushed along the rough boards, which his friends find immensely funny. Jane looks up. Lak! She jumps to her feet and runs over to him. But his greeting is not as she was hoping. "Come," he grunts, and he goes out of the room again, leading her down the stairs where three Sikhs sit around a mat. "Sit." She sits. These are important men. Even though they sit on the floor, a sense of power surrounds them.

"We are returning home to continue our work preventing the British taking over the Punjab," Lak begins.

"Can I come with you? Please … I don't want to stay here any more. I can help. You know I can help …"

Lak looks at the other men. They shake their heads. "She is British," one of them says. "She is the enemy," says another.

"But I'm not the enemy. I don't belong here. I belong with you."

Though Lak appeals on her behalf, they are immoveable. "No. We cannot trust her."

"You can trust her," says Lak. "And you will trust her to be our eyes and ears here in this city. She has already done this."

"And she betrayed you to the soldiers."

"I didn't betray you. I warned you of a trap."

"Yet Lak was almost killed."

"And I came willingly as his hostage to protect him."

"We do not trust you."

Lak has had enough now. "I trust her," he says. "We will trust her to watch her people for us. She can enter places where our people cannot go. She will hear things which will never be spoken if you or I are in the room." The three men look away. They have no more inclination to argue. Lak pulls Jane to her feet. "Come with me," he says.

He takes her outside where they only have to walk to the end of the street and turn the corner to arrive at the dockside. Several ships are in process of being unloaded or loaded; and several more are anchored out in the river. A rowing boat with two passengers pushes away from the stairs and heads towards a large ship with three masts. The ship is so big that it remains motionless in the small river waves that make every other vessel rock and sway as if impatient to be off somewhere. "That will be me, very soon," he says, pointing to the boat. "This is the ship that will take us back home. We leave when the tide turns tonight." He looks down at her. "I will be sad to leave you," he says. "But happy if you will be our friend and tell us what you hear in London." Suri nods. "Yes," she whispers. "But one day I will come home to you." Lak nods and squeezes her hand.

Lak tries to send her away, but she won't go until she has seen the ship sail. She waits until, much later in the day, Lak and his companions take a boat to their ship, and at last the vessel raises its anchor and begins to move on the tide and the river current towards the sea, her sails blossoming like spring in the bare trees of the masts. And Suri becomes Jane again. A girl alone in a part of the city where all strangers are prey.

THE UNWANTED SPY

Sad but determined, she finds her own way back to the White Bear. She remembers this when she is much older, and she thinks that never in her life has she done anything so brave and stupid as this walk – a young girl wandering on her own through alleys and streets that even the bravest watchman will not enter. It must be her innocence that protects her; also, that her clothes are not too rich; and that anyone looking at her can see that she is determinedly on her way somewhere and marching through their lives without seeing them. She will carry no tales from these streets.

She's tired when she finally arrives in Piccadilly. She walks through the archway of the White Bear and straight into the tap room, where she finds James and the General exactly as she expected – seated in a corner with cards and wine on the table in front of them. The General sees her first and leaps to his feet in excitement. "Jane, my girl! What happened? Are you hurt? Where have you been? How did you escape from that evil

Hindu?" He nearly knocks over the table – and does send three stools skittering across the flag-stoned floor – as he rushes to embrace her. And even James, following shyly behind, takes her in his arms and hugs her.

They sit her down and make her tell them everything that has happened. "That Colonel wants to see you," James says. "Indeed he does," shouts the General. "But he can wait a little while longer." And they call for pie and oysters for Jane – oh, very well, just a little if it's too much for you, dear – and some refreshing drink for all of them. By the time these essentials have been attended to, it is nearly dark.

"Do we think the Colonel can wait another day?" says the General.

"I'm certain of it." James hates disagreement above all else.

But they are not to have their way. Red coats in the doorway are making their way towards them. And inside one of these coats is the Colonel. He pretends to be pleased to have come upon them accidentally. "So you've returned, young woman. Excellent." He picks up one of the stools the General knocked over and sits himself down at their table. "When were you going to come to see me?"

Jane does not allow herself to be intimidated. "We were about to set off this very minute, were we not, Uncle?" The General nods vigorously. "So good of you to save us the trouble," says Jane. The Colonel takes her meaning correctly. She is telling him she doesn't care what he thinks.

"I wonder if you could possibly find a few minutes to inform me more fully about the events of the past few hours, madam?"

"Of course, Colonel," says Jane, in as sprightly and helpful fashion as she can. "At your pleasure."

The Colonel's pleasure is now, but he is content to move to a private parlour in the inn, to save them the trouble of removing to his house.

"I have another communication for your attention."

He is about to lay the paper on the table in front of her, but notices the small puddles of wine and passes it to her instead. She studies it for a long time.

"What's the problem, madam?" he asks sharply.

She shakes her head. "Nothing. Just a minute." What she is really thinking is whether to translate what she reads, which would endanger Lak's friends, or whether to invent some harmless nothing and pretend that she is reading it. Unfortunately, she is not as expert a liar as she thinks – or hopes. The Colonel reaches out to take the page back from her. "Just another moment," she says.

"My young lady, it seems to me that you have a decision to make. And that is, to make up your pretty mind whose side are you on." He pulls the page from her hands and is about to put it back in his pocket. But he changes his mind and gives it back to her as he stands up. "I have made a copy and will get a translation elsewhere. If you wish to help us, and your translation matches the other, then I will be very happy to talk with you. Until then, when you are able to set my mind at rest, I shall say farewell." He stands. "Gentlemen." He bows briskly and marches from the room; the sound of his boots echo on the wooden floor as if a company of goblins runs alongside him. And then there is silence in the room. The General clears his throat.

"What does he mean, my dear?"

PART THREE

LEAVING LONDON

It is a difficult few days. The affection that the General has developed for Jane – this strange new person in his life – is severely strained when he learns what she has been doing, and that she admits that she doesn't really know where she belongs.

For his part, he is unable to imagine anything but complete devotion to King and Country – the country being England, of course. James, too, is if anything even more rooted not only in the Country, but the countryside of his native Wiltshire, since he has scarcely ever journeyed more than twenty-five miles or so from his home, and finds London exciting, terrifying, and deeply disturbing. He enjoys being able to talk about his visits to London, but when he's there he can hardly wait to return to the familiar chalk downs, forest, and meadows of his true home. He stares at the mighty Thames from one of its bridges, excitedly watches the dozens of boats of all sizes crossing and journeying up and down – and thinks of the busy, clear, fresh streams of home; of the trailing water-weed; the darting fish; the water that you can actually drink. This last thought as he shudders at the sight of what he is sure is a dead body knocking against the pillars of a landing stage on the London river. The General, of course, has fought for his country, and his life continues to be worth living mainly through the memories and the tales he can tell of those great and stirring times.

So neither of them have the mental equipment to understand any other loyalty than total devotion to England – or possibly to Greater Britain (though the Scots and the Welsh are very hard to understand). After all, they simply don't know anything else.

But Jane's loyalties are confused.

She only knows that to help one person means to betray another. She can think of nothing she can do which will not bring harm to somebody.

And she doesn't want to leave London. It's as if going away would leave a job unfinished – as if she has some kind of responsibility to stay in the city. But she also knows that there's nothing she can do. Lak is gone. The Colonel and his people don't trust her. She certainly has no wish to remain anywhere close to her Grandmother. So she allows herself to be woken very early and bundled into a morning stagecoach – the General's and James's horses not yet recovered from their ride – leaving the White Bear for Bath. Dawn has not yet stroked her roseate fingers across the sky etc., etc. And probably won't because it's a dull day and it might even rain.

Climbing into the coach is already a squeeze, since the coach has started in St. Giles, at the Boar and Castle, before stopping at the Green Man and Still in Oxford Street. There isn't really room for another three passengers, but James agrees to ride outside, and Jane is slim and can be compressed into the last remaining space in the coach, between the General and a mother travelling with her daughters to take the waters at Bath. Naturally, they've no interest in the supposedly health-giving properties of the water. They journey in search of wealthy husbands. The mother is as thin in body as she is in spirit. Unfortunately for the other passengers in the coach, her daughters take after their dear, late father, who, although a good-humoured man, and generally content with one slice of pie, was always considerably more contented by the addition of a second – to keep the first slice company, he used to say, since he knew what it was to be lonely, and wished his pie to find the same happiness as he had when first meeting the girls' beloved mother. In short, there is little room to breathe inside the coach. At least the day is not too warm. Jane rather envies James and his outside seat.

The day goes on for a hundred years, and finally they arrive in Newbury, where they climb stiffly down while horses and drivers are changed. The General has had enough of stagecoach travel, but James says they should remain with the coach until Marlborough, where they can hire a trap for the last miles to Nightride Priory.

They should have made their own way.

They are late, of course. The roads are in better condition than they have been, but the coach has still not managed to keep going at the desired eight miles per hour. In fact, on the lonely stretch of road between Hungerford and Marlborough, they are scarcely travelling faster than they could walk. Jane has entered a dream state, halfway between waking and a restless sleep. She likes this half-world. It means she can play with reality. She smiles secretly as she sees the faces of her travelling companions metamorphose into something that's very like them, but different. The bony mother becomes a yappy lapdog – though an unusually tall one. And her daughters are revealed to be – not piglets, no. They're ferrets. Funny to find something so thin and energetic in creatures so large and lardy as these girls.

The coach jolts and stops, and Jane

is shaken out of her dream-world. Have they arrived somewhere? Everyone is climbing down from inside and outside the coach. Still in a confused and half-asleep state, she, too, clambers down, blinking herself awake. A man sits on a horse, pointing at the coachman. What a strange shape his hand is. That's because it's a pistol. *Ah,* Jane thinks, *this is a highwayman. How exciting.* She moves slowly along to a position where she can see better, from where the highwayman is no longer silhouetted against the light.

"Thank you for your co-operation, gentlefolk," he is saying. "I would be much obliged if you would place the contents of your pockets, purses, and such, down on the ground before you. Quite slowly if you please. And I'm quite sure that it's unnecessary to remind gentlefolk of your intelligence that I have not one, but two hands, and am lucky enough to possess a pistol for each of them."

Jane thinks, *I should be terrified. Why am I not frightened? His voice ... something is familiar about him. I have seen him before. Where have I seen him before?*

She remembers. She steps forward. Immediately, as if on a spring, the pistol in his right hand swings to point at her. "Have a care, young madam," he says. "I should hate to spoil your beautiful dress." She hates herself for being pleased that he noticed. It's not a very grand dress, but it is a new one.

"Shame on you, sir," she calls.

"Yes, yes," he says. "You're not the first to say such a thing, but we all have to live. I simply behave in a manner more direct than most."

"You were once my protector," she continues. "And I admired you. But now I see you are no more than a robber who talks too much."

That's got him, she thinks. She keeps her gaze firmly on his face. Above the mask his expression is blank. Then, slowly, a laugh appears around his eyes. "Well, well. Yes, I remember now. But that was a different coach and a different day." Exactly. It was the day when Jane first arrived at Nightride Priory, when the General and James behaved like hooligans, pretending to rob the coach she was in.

"I see," said Jane. "So you change from lion to lizard in a day. How is anyone to trust a person such as you?"

He laughed aloud. "It's in the nature of your highwayman to be untrustworthy, my lady."

"But I thought better of you, and now you have disappointed me."

His pistol still points steadily at her. But meanwhile, seeing that the robber's attention is distracted, the coachman moves, perhaps reaching for a weapon. The spell is broken. The highwayman fires at the coachman – but it seems to Jane that he is aiming well above his head – turns his horse around, and gallops off across the cleared ground beside the road to disappear into the trees. Suddenly Jane is surrounded by jabbering passengers. Their words jumble together in a single wash of sound, and she feels very tired. Above the babble she hears James's enthusiastic voice, "Excellent sport! Our very own warrior princess, by gad …"

THE VAULTS

"It doesn't look at all ghostly to me." Jane's mood is very down-to-earth today. Normally she's happy to see mysteries everywhere, but since her return from London she has become inclined to trust nothing but what she can see with her own eyes. The twins are different. They're bored by the world they see in front of them every day and they desperately want to find something different and more interesting under the surface. They're overjoyed to have Jane back with them, because with her they can explore the Priory and its ruins and hidden corners without being chased away.

"Of course not, nothing ever looks ghostly in the sunshine," says Charles, who fancies himself the more practical of the two, being the boy. (It's time you knew their names. The twins are Charles and Charlotte, which seemed nicely assonant to their parents at the time of their birth, but which has naturally caused endless confusion amongst acquaintances and relatives ever since.) "But just wait until dark," he adds.

"We've seen her, you know," Charlotte says.

"Who?" Jane doesn't believe anything nowadays.

"The Grey Lady. She's real. We've seen her walking among the ruins."

"We're hoping she will show us where she buried the treasure," says Charles, and recites a well-worn local verse. "Where faithful dog, wise owl, grey lady lie/there's gold for truest heart to find."

"How do you know there's any treasure? How do you know this ghost buried it even if there is?"

"Oh, don't be so ill-humoured, Jane," Charlotte reaches out and takes her hand. "Maybe there is a treasure; maybe there isn't. But what fun can we have unless we look?"

"We'd have nothing but grass and sheep," says Charles, waving his arm to show the countryside around them. And indeed, there seems to be very little else. They've walked from the Priory and are atop the chalk downs overlooking their village – and from where they stand, there is, as Charles says, nothing to see but grass dotted with sheep.

At twilight that evening they meet in the ruins. Spring is on its way, but for now the night still falls early enough, and their excuses for going outside don't have to be elaborate or persuasive. They have brought lanterns – and Charles also has his treasured tinderbox, along with two candles he has borrowed from the kitchen.

It was once a doorway, but a collapsing wall has concealed it and mostly blocked it – but there is a space wide enough to squeeze through if you're small enough. They're all three excited, all wondering whether they really want to be this brave, but not daring to be the first to suggest going home. And so, like a Sunday outing that nobody wants, but where nobody will be the first to say so, they push their way through, one after another, and find themselves inside a passageway. Their flickering lanterns are most useful at casting frightening shadows of themselves and seem to tell them very little about the room they're in. "Wait until your eyes get used to the dark," says Jane, remembering her explorations of the caves by the village where she used to live.

It's just as well that they haven't rushed on into the darkness, since soon they see that they stand at the top of a staircase. Charles turns grinning to the girls. "The vaults," he says. "Treasure is always in the vaults."

Slowly, they feel their way down the stairs – some of which are crumbling, but most of which are in good condition. "I expect nobody has been here for more than two hundred years," says Charlotte. There's a note of awe in her voice.

"What's the story of the treasure?" Jane asks. "Why was it buried?"

"The stories are different. Some say it was in the civil war. The house was on the side of the King, and Cromwell's troops marched on it after the Battle at Newbury and took it. The family had to flee and hid their treasure. But they never came back to find it again. Maybe they were all killed. But some stories say it's older, from the time of the Wars of the Roses, when Henry Tudor marched this way to fight King Richard. It would still have been a priory, then, so maybe the monks hid the treasure for someone else. Or maybe it was their own."

"This is a lovely vault, but don't you think that if you were burying treasure, you might put it somewhere harder to find? I mean not just in the cellar?" Jane says. The twins cough together. She's right, of course. Charles insists on exploring some more, but they don't find anything, though they're excited to find how untouched the room seems to be. But it's only one chamber, one cellar. They find no passages leading from it.

"Let's go now and think about what to do next. We can always come back," Charlotte suggests.

They squeeze back into the open air and sneak their way across the dew-damp, meadowed grass towards the house. They don't see the grey figure watching them from behind a crumbling doorway. And if they had caught a glimpse and turned back to be sure, they would have found nothing there.

NIGHT CREATURES

While the young people discuss where they would hide treasure if it were something they had to do, let us use the magic of ink to visit London. Ink the colour of night, since night it is, and a suitable colour for its creatures – people like our lawyer, Hardfist. He has no need to accustom himself to the dark. It's the daylight that ignites his fears. Bright daylight, when all can be seen and there are no shadows to conceal from the adroitness of the right hand what the sinister, left, hand is doing. *Sinister* – Latin, "the left" – carries its meaning of evil because for most people their left side is their weaker side, and so the side where the devil has most chance of overpowering us. Hardfist is left-handed and has no fear of the devil, whom he regards as a colleague.

At this moment he is striding along Fleet Street, which looks rather festive, since the evening is warm, and the shops are lantern-lit to catch the last of the day's strolling crowds, though now the lights are going out as the streets become empty. He has had an idea, has asked a few questions amongst people of his acquaintance, and is now acting upon the information he has persuaded from them.

He enters the shop of a tailor and dressmaker and calls for the owner. He wastes no time on pleasantries. "General Headlong has an outstanding account with you," he announces and places a guinea on the counter. Surprised, the tailor agrees that while such things are naturally confidential, this might be the case. "I would like you to call in this account immediately," says Hardfist. "In full. I am a lawyer and will assist you." He places another guinea on the counter.

The tailor hesitates. "I fear it might be difficult for the General to pay the entire account at once," he suggests. Hardfist reveals a tooth – it's almost as if he were attempting a smile. "Indeed," he says.

Soon Hardfist is once again in the rookeries of St. Giles. He passes through the filthy, narrow alleys and courtyards with a mixture of distaste and familiarity. Yes, his work brings him into contact with these people, but more important is that, try as he might, he cannot forget that he is himself a child of the slums, and has escaped through luck and cunning. At fourteen he was the same as everyone else – except that he noticed more of what went on around him than most. And one of the things he noticed in his frequent appearances in court (he is lucky to be alive) was that whatever the result of the case, lawyers would be paid.

Not much later he had the moment of luck which transformed his life. He robbed a house – yet another. But the haul was much greater than he expected. He had stolen enough to live for years, if he were careful. Unlike most of his companions, he was quick-witted enough to take advantage of the moment. Not only was he not caught, but he invested in himself, bought expensive clothes, and spent his days watching trials in and around the inns and courts of law, where he bought or stole as much knowledge as he could. After a while he simply set himself up with a brass plaque and let it be known that he was available. His second great stroke of luck was that one of his first clients was a gentleman who was being pursued for unpaid bills. Hardfist not only rescued the gentleman, but bankrupted the predatory wine merchant. After that, the word of his skill spread, and his future was set. Although he remains poor, he usually makes enough to live on. But he still needs the help of some of the people he knows from his childhood. He tries, but can never quite shake off the slime of the slums and of the scavengers on the beaches of the river at low tide.

You will remember this room. You have seen it before. It's dark, so you won't recognize the staircase, its chipped steps, and the stains which are probably blood, but you know the face that looks up as Hardfist pushes his way into the room, even though the flame that clings to the remaining stub of the single tallow candle flickers mightily. Robert, our actor. His fortunes have not improved since last we saw him.

Seeing Hardfist, he raises his arm towards him. "Stay," he croaks.

"What's that?" Hardfist walks over to him. "What have you got there? A pistol. Well, I'll be damned – yes, probably I am. And where did you get that? Stole it backstage in some theatre? Get up. Stand up, I say, or I leave you to starve."

Robert pulls himself to his feet and gazes at Hardfist, swaying slightly with weariness and hunger. Hardfist lays five shilling coins on the table. "Get yourself some food, and retrieve your stolen horse from the Golden Cross. I will shortly have more riding for you." And he melts back into the darkness.

In Cavendish Square they are not so careful with candles. Jane's grandmother has guests to dinner and, since she only ever consorts with people who can be of some advantage to her, she is keen to show that she has no need for household economies. This is as true as everything else in her life, which is to say scarcely at all. The evening has cost a great deal and she and her servants will live off bread and mutton soup for the remainder of the month. But we are all actors, as she has often said, only some are better than others.

Hardfist is not welcome. In spite of the expensive suit that he still manages to maintain, he carries a whiff of the Underworld, and Grandmother does not wish her guests to see him. She bustles into the room where Hardfist has been permitted to wait for the last half an hour.

"What is it?" she snaps. "It must be quick, or come back tomorrow."

"I will come straight to the point," he says.

"Please do."

"I have a way of persuading the General to give up your granddaughter at once." Her eyebrows arch. "I have a tailor's bill with which I can make him bankrupt and homeless, since I know he has not the means to pay it. I need only your ladyship's permission to proceed..."

"Excellent. Do it."

ANCIENT PLANS

Jane decides to find out what the General knows about the buried treasure. She has been thinking it over again and again all through the night, and it occurs to her that, for all they know, the General might already have found the treasure – and even spent all the money.

"There is no treasure, my dear," the General smiles. "I wish there were, but we have all wasted a great deal of time searching and we've found nothing. Somebody would have found something in two hundred years if there were anything to find." He pats her hand consolingly. "It's just a story. Every old house has stories of buried treasure."

"And who's the Grey Lady?"

"Another story, I fear. Have you seen her?"

"No. Not yet. Have you?"

"No. Even though when I was your age I spent whole nights watching for her. But if you're determined to waste your time, then come with me. I have something you will need."

He takes her into the library (a room

full of books which have not been opened for a generation). After a few minutes rummaging through a chest of wide, thin drawers, he pulls out two large sheets of paper and lays them on the table. "Here," he says. "This is a view of the priory before it was ruined. And here," he puts the other sheet on top, "is a plan. We are here." He points. She looks. "So these are the ruins," she says. "What's this? Isn't that just a field?"

"The house is only a small part of what was once here, d'you see. The priory church and its cloisters were in that field, but there's nothing left now. All that useful stone taken to build houses all over the county. It's like an old battlefield now. The vultures picked everything clean. Grass grown over what was left. I'm sorry, my dear. There's really no hope."

But Jane's only thought is, *we've been looking in the wrong place.*

The twins are not convinced. "You want us to take shovels to a field?" Jane has never heard Charles contemptuous before. Even Charlotte wears an amused expression.

"If that's where the treasure is, that's where we must look," Jane snaps. "You think we should only look where it's in easy? Would you hide your treasure where any passer-by could simply pick it up, as from a market stall?"

"At least we could look in daylight," Charlotte suggests. Charles doesn't like being contradicted. "What's the good of that?" he barks. "So that if we find anything the world will know at once? Why don't we invite the county to take the clothes from our backs while we're about it?"

Charlotte simply sighs. There's no arguing with him when he's like this.

"We should ask the Grey Lady to help," Jane says. At which the twins snort in unison.

In the afternoon, they take the plan of the priory to the field, matching the still-existing walls to the plan so that they can mark out where the church once stood. "There's a dew pond right in the middle of the nave," Charles observes. "The monks would have wet feet …"

And at night they return with shovels

and shrouded lanterns. "Like grave-robbers," Charlotte says. "Yes!" shouts Jane. "Perhaps that's what we are. Perhaps the treasure is hidden in a grave!"

"And I suppose the Grey Lady will shortly appear to show us where to dig." Charles is very caustic today.

"Perhaps it's her grave. She guards the treasure …"

"By remaining hidden and never appearing?"

Charlotte shrieks. Alarmed and slightly frightened, they turn to see her pointing to the place where the existing house meets the old ruins.

"The Grey Lady. I saw her."

Whether she did or no, we shall never know, for a badger chooses that moment to waddle across the field from exactly the place at which Charlotte points. "Hello, Grey Lady," says Charles. "You know, I think we're all mad. There is no Grey Lady. There is no treasure. We're just children in a field at night."

He turns and begins to stomp angrily away. The girls hear a cry and a splash. He has fallen into the dew pond, almost invisible in the darkness. He stands, up to his knees in water and still holding his shovel. He doesn't know whether to be angry or to laugh. Charlotte and Jane try very hard to hold in their giggles, waiting to take a cue from him, but it's too much. They break out into howls of laughter, and even Charles has to see that it's funny. He slams the shovel down through the water in mock petulance. To his surprise, the shovel does not stop at his feet, but goes further into the soft ground. He pushes harder down on it in an attempt to lever himself out of the pond, but the shovel sinks deeper into the mud. In the end, the laughing girls pull him out of the water, and he has to leave the shovel where it is. Still, Jane is not going to give up the search.

THE HIGHWAY

Robert is equipped with solicitor's letters, a new message for the General, and his pistol, returned with a sneer by Hardfist. He is riding at no great speed along the road to Wiltshire, enjoying the knowledge that, at least for a few days, he has money in his pocket and a place in the world. He crosses Hounslow Heath, and he thinks how lonely the road can be. For a mile or two, he sees no other travellers but a single coach. He thinks how vulnerable we are on the road, and how easily robbed.

The shiver down his spine is of fear for his own safety, but he begins to think. What if he were not the victim but the cause of fear? Why should he not be the one in command? He remembers his thoughts of becoming a highwayman in reality, and his actor's eye sees himself charming and deadly, a figure to be admired and desired. *By gosh, people would be proud to be robbed by me!* And why not change that "would" to "will"? He has the correct clothing. He has the necessary pistol. So he is thinking as he rides slowly across the Heath. So he dreams as he rides along.

But it is on the next day, as he enters Savernake Forest, that his dream hardens. It has rained in the night, and a fine drizzle still sparkles and thickens the air as the sun struggles to appear. Two young men approach at a gallop on their way towards London, forcing him off the road and splashing him with mud. He hears them laugh as they ride into the distance, and the anger of the turning worm rises in him. He rides into the trees to compose himself. It slowly becomes clear to him that now he is waiting for a traveller worth robbing to appear on the road.

Of course, as an apprentice lion, he is fated to bite at far more than he could possibly chew. He hears a coach approaching. Without pausing to think, he rides into the road and raises his pistol. "Stand and deliver!" he cries. The coach – having the additional self-importance of carrying His Majesty's Mail – doesn't even pause. The coachman whips out at him as they pass, and knocks off his hat. He is left with nothing but the laughter of the coachman and outside passengers as a bitter garnish to this first attempt to crown himself King of the Road. And a rising anger at being downtrodden yet again.

He retrieves his hat, washes off the mud in the cleanest puddle he can find, and readies himself for the next traveller. "King of the road?" he says to himself. "Then be a king. Not Robert the actor, but Robert the Bruce. Prince Hal ... I am King Henry V, and this is my Agincourt." Stirred to the very core, he raises his arm above his head to the sound of cheering troops. (Imaginary cheering troops, naturally.)

"Stand and deliver!" A clear clarion call to another unfortunate carriage passing along the road.

"Deliver? Certainly, if that's what you want! Here's your delivery, squire." Two sturdy countrymen drive a cart to market. Behind them on the cart, cabbages, three lambs, two baskets containing eggs – with which they fearlessly pelt the bold highwaymen. Robert wheels his startled horse around and canters off down the road, yellow yolk smearing his only good coat, front and back.

He hides himself in the trees, using wet leaves to clean himself as best he can, and tries not to cry. One final attempt. He will not be beaten. He is made of sterner stuff. For he is of ancient lineage – descended from the family of knights who came over with the Conqueror! This is his destiny!

"Stand and deliver!"

A woman and her two young daughters stand and quiver in the fear of what he will do to them. This is more like it. And what's more, an opportunity to show himself chivalrous.

"You have nothing to fear from me, Madam, but I shall require the contents of your purse."

"'Tis all we have, good sir," the woman's voice shakes. Robert the King of the Highway tips his hat. "I fear 'tis the luck of the draw, madam. We are all needy. Thank you for your kindness and I wish you a more fortunate onward journey. Ladies." Once again he touches his hat in salute and canters off down the road (he is not a good enough horseman to manage a gallop, particularly not on such roads). But he can't escape her cry,

"Shame on you, sir. For shame!"

Later he slows to examine his winnings. He has gained two shillings and four pence. And an enemy for life, he supposes. He hopes he won't encounter them again.

DRY GRASS

"Mr. Charles and Miss Charl–" Darkling is doing his best to keep up the proprieties, but since Jane has returned from London, the twins have been in and out of the Priory at will, as if they, too, lived there. They push past him as he announces them to Jane and the General, who are at their breakfast.

"It's gone. It's dried up!" Charles squeaks in a most unmanly manner.

"Steady there, young man," says the General. "Think about your message and deliver it clearly."

"The water …"

"What water, my friend?"

"The dew pond. The water has drained away …"

The General snorts. "I expect it's just dried up."

"But everything else is soaked. It rained in the night. It should be full. I think we put a hole in it and it's drained out into something underneath."

"Is that what you think?"

"Yes, sir."

He has delivered his news. He is deflated now. He and Charlotte stand in the doorway, not quite sure what to do next. The General has just realized what he said.

"You put a hole in it? What do you mean by that?"

Jane quickly tried to save any awkwardness. "We were exploring yesterday afternoon. We're looking for the treasure, Uncle."

The General looks at the eager young faces and doesn't have the heart to disappoint them. He harrumphs gently and, muttering something about keeping the horses waiting, he shambles from the room.

"Where faithful dog, wise owl, grey lady lie/there's gold for truest heart to find," Darkling breathes the familiar lines.

"Yes," say the twins. "We all know the words. But what do they mean?"

"I'm sure I don't know. You brought the verse to mind, nothing more, young sir." And he whispers his way from the room.

He is more helpful a little later as they collect shovels from the corner of the stable.

"I would not like to see you dig up the meadow. Go to Mrs. Pitcher. Ask her to show you the graven owl." And, having uttered this mystery, he dissolves into shadow once more.

A horseman canters up the drive to the house and hammers on the door. He doesn't see Jane and the twins, but she gives out a sob of fear at the sight of his dark figure. "It's the man who took me to London, I'm sure of it. My kidnapper." She runs from the sight to the kitchen yard and the protecting influence of Mrs. Pitcher.

She is right, and the General, being in the house, cannot escape. The visitor is most forceful in his demands and will accept no delay, but must see the General immediately. Robert is acting at his best. But it is not simply an act, for he has the letters and messages from Hardfist to support him.

"General, you must give up the girl," he declares.

"But I do not wish it; and I believe it is her wish to remain with me and not to return to her grandmother."

"Nevertheless, it will go hard with you if you do not comply with our ... suggestions."

"Do you threaten me, sir?"

"Indeed I do. There is still the matter of the Lady and the Burgundy ..." The General flaps his hands, as if to say "Pshaw ..."

"And if that matter no longer disturbs you," Robert continues, "we have a more pressing matter to bring to your attention." With an air of triumph, he produces the letter from Hardfist. "You have a rather large account outstanding with Messrs Threadman and Sons ..."

"I think you'll find they are the most patient people in the world." The General is not frightened by this.

"I think you'll find otherwise, sir. They desire immediate payment in full, and have already applied to the courts for an order of bankruptcy against you, since they have no confidence that you can pay."

The General has turned pale.

"I will return for the girl this afternoon. Have her packed and ready to leave. Good day to you, sir." He sweeps theatrically from the room, passing Darkling, who has of course heard every word from the other side of the door.

"A pickle, sir," he wafts.

"Thankee, no. I've only now had breakfast."

"It seems in a pickle is where we find ourselves, sir."

"There's no money, Darkling. None at all. We should have to sell the house." The General stares at the floorboards, which he can see through the holes in the carpet at his feet. "Why are they going to such lengths to have the girl in their grasp?"

"I fancy it is her inheritance, sir."

"What's that?"

"If you remember, sir. Her father was Baronet Bridgeman. When he married your sister, he renounced the title in favour of his brother before departing – to hide away, it seems, in India. On the brother's recent sad death, the title willy-nilly returned to the girl's father, and on his sad demise, the girl inherits. She is a minor. Whoever has care of the girl also has care of the Bridgeman fortune."

"But dammit all, I think I've grown quite fond of the little thing. I ain't going to give her up to that harridan, Darkling."

"Your step-mother, General …"

The General becomes uncharacteristically animated and decisive. It's almost as if he were a military man again. "She's a vicious old … woman. Always has been. We must find a solution. I will talk with James. He always has splendid ideas."

Darkling struggles to conceal a smile at the thought of the wisdom of James. "Very good, sir."

THE COLD, COLD GROUND

"The Graven Owl? Well. He's never asked that before. You'll have to move some boxes, mind." Mrs. Pitcher is only slightly put out at their request. She trusts that Darkling always knows best, and so never questions his judgement.

"You'll need lanterns," she says.

She leads them through a maze of narrow passages in the cellars. (This is not just an expression. Look at a plan of the priory cellars and you will see that it really is a maze, probably continuing the shape of passages created a thousand years before the priory was built – perhaps more – designed to protect an ancient mystery.)

At last they arrive at a storeroom protected by wooden gates, which she unlocks with one of the dozens of keys hanging in a bunch from her waist. "It's a long time since this was opened," she says – and indeed, the hinges are stiff and creak mightily.

When they have moved aside the stacks of empty boxes and rolled away the barrel, they see by the light of their lantern that there is a doorway. And in the thickness of the wall near the arch is cut the figure of an owl. It's a little rough, but done with care. Not quite a sculpture, but more than graffiti. "What now?" they ask.

"The door is not locked. We have no key for it. Open it and see."

They enter what seems to be a large area, divided by vaulted arches. Stones have fallen and the ceiling has collapsed in places. The shivering light from their lanterns shines back at them from water on the flagstone floor. Charles is the first to realize where they are. "This is the crypt under the church. This is where the dew pond drained down." He pushes further forward. Charlotte shrieks. "Grey Lady! I saw the Grey Lady."

But she is wrong. Although they are all slightly shaky with fear, Jane bravely walks further into the crypt to touch the figure in the shadows.

"They're tombs. Graves," she says. "All the people who were buried under the church. Look, a knight in armour. A bishop ..."

"It's like a chess game," Charlotte giggles, slightly hysterical. "Where's the queen?"

There's a long silence. Jane speaks, a strange catch in her voice. "She's here. This is the Grey Lady."

Above them, across the meadow and the road, and a few miles away our brave highwayman – not our actor, but the real one – is about to make the biggest mistake of his life. You will remember him. He saved Jane from the General's attack on her coach when she first arrived in England; you saw him again holding up her carriage as she returned from London. He is feeling good this morning. The sun is shining. Spring is in the air. His past few days fishing in the bountiful streams of the coaching roads have been productive. He fancies that one more such haul will see him able to put his feet up for a few weeks.

Just one last haul. Whenever you read or hear someone make this promise to themselves you know that something terrible will happen. The brave soldier will die as he packs his bags ready to travel home after this last patrol; the missionary will be captured by a hostile tribe on this final journey before he retires to the country, his thatched cottage, and his family's fire, slippered feet, and comforting evening pipe; the gallant explorer will return just one more time to the forest in search of hidden gold – and meet his end at the hands of a fearsome beast, or angry natives. And what of a highwayman, planning one last adventure?

Justice Thomas, on the other hand, is not feeling good, and is not enjoying another day aboard a coach. The road is rough. He is tired. He will not reach Exeter tonight, a place he has no real wish to go, but where he will oversee the assize courts. Each rut and pit in the road makes him more unhappy and increasingly short-tempered. His companions do nothing to brighten his mood, being a captain of infantry and two rather dull gentlemen inside, and half a dozen of the captain's soldiers outside. These are intended for the protection of the Judge, but they are dismal company and he doubts both their necessity and their ability. The captain, on the other hand, is looking forward to some sport, and has told his soldiers to cover their uniforms in the hope that some unsuspecting bandit will fall into his trap.

"Closer. Closer with the lantern." Jane traces the outline of the tomb with her hands, almost caressing the stone form of the dead woman in front of her.

"How do you know?" Once certain of the existence of the Grey Lady, Charles has now become the most sceptical.

"Because the tomb says, 'Elizabeth Grey'." She pauses, as if she only now notices what she has said. "How strange. Elizabeth is my mother's name. This Elizabeth died in 1466, and she was thirty-four years old. I wonder what she died of."

"There's a puppy at her feet," says Charlotte.

"Faithful Dog …" Charles mutters. "Grey Lady. Where's the Wise Owl?"

The base of the tomb is carved all around. Eagerly they move the lantern, stroking and peering at the stone figures. There are deer, apple trees, more dogs – but there is no owl. "Perhaps it's the wrong Lady Grey," says Jane. Her voice is heavy with disappointment.

They stand up and look around – as much as this is possible in a crumbling crypt lit only by flickering lanterns. "Here it is," says Charlotte, quietly. Above the tomb, like the head of a bed, is another scene showing the Garden of Eden. And in one of the trees sits an owl.

"Excellent. But where's the treasure?" says Charles. "If there is any treasure." Their excitement drains away once more.

"What am I to do, James? What am I to do?"

James takes a thoughtful draft of his wine. "Time to break open the hidden fighting fund, I think." The General shakes his head slowly. "Gone. All gone." He looks sideways at his friend, and, speaking rather shyly, says, "I don't suppose … it's simply a tailor's bill … I don't …" But James is already shaking his head regretfully. "Sorry to say, your not supposing is right. You know I would help if I could, old man, but I am in your boat, but for the last straw. My credit is all used up. I scratch from week to week, loaf by loaf, bottle by glass …"

The General sighs. He had known this, but felt he had to ask. It's never too late to hope for a miracle, and foolish not to look when you need one.

"Why has this stepmother taken against you?"

"Oh, she always hated me. My father never truly recovered from the dying of my mother, and when he married again … well, 'twas a mistake, and she did for him in the end."

"Gracious! Poison?"

The General laughs at the wonder on his friend's face. "Nothing so tidy. Wore him out until he faded away. Horrible harridan. Just five years, and he was in the cold, cold ground." He brightens. "But she didn't get the Priory. The house is mine."

"If you can pay this bill."

Gloom descends on the drinking gents once more. James gives a cynical little laugh. "Well, we can always take to the highway and rob a carriage or two," he says.

Somebody is already about that very thing – though not to the benefit of the

General. Our elegant young man waits restlessly in the bushes at the edge of the forest. His heart is no longer in this. He would rather go now to the nearest inn and rest in the corner by the fire. But he has set himself a task, and he will carry it through.

He hears horses, and the rumble of wheels, and readies himself. But the vehicle rounding the bend in the road is a farmer's wagon, his family and friends walking alongside. Instead of excitement, our friend feels frustration. They move slowly, and it takes an age for them to pass and disappear from view. Lost in thought, he almost doesn't hear the coach, soon afterwards. But there it is, making much noise as it struggles to keep up some speed on the rutted, pitted road. He rides out into the road to block its way. But what's this?

"Aha!" A triumphant cry from a passenger leaning out of the window. "Take him!"

Six muskets appear from nowhere, each levelled and steadying their aim at him. Considering discretion the better part of valour ("He who fights and runs away, lives to fight another day.") he turns rapidly. His horse, startled, rears up. He doesn't fall – though for a few seconds the danger is great, and he seems to hang for a moment, like a stone thrown high but in the end unable to withstand the call of gravity. At last man and horse recover and gallop to the safety of the trees. He hears a whistling near his ear. His hat flies away. But soon he is safe; panting and sweat-drenched. He pauses to listen. To his relief, it seems the soldiers are not following him. He can't know this, but the judge is already impatient enough and will accept no further delay in his journey. Slowly our friend walks on through the forest, feeling his breathing ease while the sweat dries under his shirt.

But his story is not yet ended.

Jane can't resist reaching out to touch the stone owl – she feels that only then will she believe that it's real. So she passes her fingers over the sculpted bird.

It wobbles.

The surprised sound she makes is almost like an owl. She grips the stone bird by its head and pulls gently. The owl is carved in relief on a piece of stone about the size of her hand. The whole piece comes away, revealing a cavity behind. Charles lifts the lantern, but none of them is tall enough to see into the space. "Help me up," says Jane, and begins to clamber onto the Grey Lady.

"We shouldn't …" Charlotte begins.

"Charlie, she's been dead three hundred and fifty years. I don't think she'll notice," Charles says. He helps Jane to climb on to the tomb and passes her his lantern. She peers at the hole and reaches her hand inside. There is no sound in the crypt. Not even the sound of breathing. She withdraws her hand, which is now holding a small bundle – it might be a purse, or just a cloth wrapped around something. Carefully she climbs down, Charles guiding her feet.

"The treasure," she breathes, excitedly. But she hasn't dared unwrap the bundle.

"It's very small," says Charlotte. "I was expecting a chest full of gold."

Jane delicately unwraps the cloth (for that's what it is). The twins can't suppress a giggle of happiness. Jane holds a handful of precious stones and small golden jewellery.

"Small, perhaps, but enough for most people to call themselves rich," says Charles.

Carefully, they return to the fallen doorway at the entrance to the crypt. They call for Mrs. Pitcher, but there is no reply.

"She must have gone back to the kitchen. No matter. We'll find our own way back." Charles speaks confidently, as he feels is his duty. He expects a few corners in cellar passageways. He doesn't know that they are in a maze.

They blunder around for quite a while but always seem to end up with their noses against a wall. Charlotte is convinced it's always the same wall, but they have no way of knowing for sure. "We should shout for help," she says. But Charles won't let her. "We'll solve this. I don't understand what's happening, but we will solve it."

"Charles, we're lost," says Jane. "We will never find our way out like this. Maybe it's the ghost of the Grey Lady. Perhaps this is how she guards her treasure."

Charles makes a noise as if to scoff at the idea. But it's not a very loud noise.

THE ROLLING, ROLLING SEA

We must collect ourselves for a little while, since there are other lives whose threads will weave together in the tapestry of this day.

Limehouse, London, perhaps two weeks ago – do you remember? With Jane you watched a ship move out upon the Thames, its sails flowering on the water until it disappeared around the bend of the stream. A friend beginning his journey of eight thousand miles. A winter voyage is a dangerous venture. Most ships deliver their cargo safely in the end, though often with tales to tell of conversations with death. But some do not. Our ship is one of those that do not.

Nobody sets out on a voyage expecting to fail. No ship's captain wants to kill himself and the greater part of his crew and passengers. But sometimes it happens all the same. The voyage starts well, on a beautiful day, perfect for sailing. Even the old captain himself – not a man normally given to thoughts on nature – stands ramrod-straight on his quarterdeck, breathes in the bright freshness of the day, and thinks, *this is why we go sailing*.

But, although the spring brings hopes of warm days and new life, it is also the time of some of the year's greatest storms. And the English Channel, for all its homely name, is a treacherous place to sail. Here, where the Channel begins to mingle with the Atlantic Ocean, is where a voyage truly begins; where home is left behind. And just here, on this night, the greatest storm of the year rips out our ship's main mast, the great tree crushing the captain and his steersman along with much of the quarterdeck. Helpless, the ship now drifts onto the Cornish rocks. Did I say "drifts"? The ship is driven and pounded onto the rocks. In a matter of minutes the great beast is reduced to a scattered collection of planks. Nothing remains of the floating tower, which seemed so invulnerable, so permanent when it gathered way along the Thames river.

Not everyone is drowned or battered to death by the storm. When the dawn comes, the survivors begin the search for each other and for any of their belongings which might have been washed ashore with them – those which have not already been taken by scavengers from the nearby villages. You mustn't blame the villagers. They are not wreckers, guiding ships aground with false lights. They are poor people, too. Why should they not gather wood and cargoes from ships wrecked on their shores? For some it makes the difference between survival and starvation. And they are not robbers or killers. Lak and his fellow survivors are left alone to manage as well as they can.

A fresh breeze is blowing, as it always does by the sea, but the sun is shining, and now it's hard to believe that this is the place where so many lives have been pounded to pieces. Surprisingly, most have survived. But 'most' means that nearly half of the crew and passengers are dead.

The survivors naturally divide into three – the Indians, the British passengers, and the surviving crew – and they depart in different directions across the moor. The Indians, in particular, find that none of the local villagers will have anything to do with them. Worse, they are spat upon and cursed as corsairs. They don't understand what this means. They don't know that Barbary pirates have been raiding these shores for centuries, kidnapping people to take as slaves to North Africa. Their misfortune is a source of joy to the villagers.

They wander the heathlands and lanes for several days until they find themselves in Falmouth. Lak has been thinking deeply since the wreck. He is as devoted as ever to fighting the British in his homeland; but there is unfinished business in his life which has been haunting him for ten years or more. Now he has walked with Death and lives again. And he fought Death so fiercely because he wanted so much to lay those ghosts of his own.

In Falmouth his friends find a ship of the East India Company bound for Bombay. Lak will not join them but promises he will not be delayed more than a month. He will find them in Amritsar. He begins to walk from Cornwall into England.

You will be wanting to return to the

ruined priory's cellars, where our heroines and hero remain in the dark, lost in the labyrinth. But you will have to be patient a little while longer, since you must first overhear an exchange between James and the General which will shed important light on General Headlong's essential nature.

They, too, remain exactly as they were when last you saw them. An inn is always their first resort when trouble strikes. The wine is comforting, for sure, but so too is the bustle around them and the feeling – you might have it, too – that other lives continue regardless of your own troubles. Somehow both of them find this soothing, and there are long periods of companionable silence where they both inspect the gleaming surface of the wine in their cups.

James has been thinking on the General's troubles. Thinking is not something that comes naturally to him, but he enjoys the sensation when an Idea springs, fully formed like Venus from the waves, out of the waters of his mind.

"You too!" he exclaims.

"What's that, old man?"

"You have the gel. That means that you have her money, just as much as her grandmother would if the gel were in her claws. You can pay all the bills you wish to! You have no troubles. All in the mind, dear General. All in the mind."

This had genuinely not occurred to the General. From the day of her arrival, and sometimes unwillingly, all he had felt was a strong sense of responsibility for Jane. He had been slow to understand why her grandmother was so desperate to get her to London; but even when the penny (as it were) had dropped, he had still not considered that the coin had two sides. If the grandmother wanted the girl because of her fortune, then if the General had the girl, he also had her fortune.

The thought wandered slowly through the wine-curtained rooms of his mind as he continued to stare into the cup before him. Suddenly he lifted his head and turned to stare keenly at James.

"Never!" he said. "We must protect the girl, and she must have her fortune entire when she is of the right age."

"Excellent sentiment. Applaud it heartily. But then you still have the little problem of the bill and the suit for bankruptcy. Without some solution you'll have nothing, dear General."

The General nods gloomily. James slaps him on the shoulder.

"Don't lose heart. I have room in my attic for your bed. As long as my own resources hold up, you will never be homeless."

And the girl in question? Three times she has listened to the boy Charles, and three times they have finished up in the same blank corner, staring at the same bricks. Now the candles in their lanterns are burning low, and soon they will be left in total darkness with no hope at all of finding their own way out. She has kept silent, but she is beginning to feel that there is something more to this – something more than their ignorance of the cellar's geography.

"We should call Mrs. Pitcher for help," she says. Charles is determined that he knows better, but the girls' superior sense wins in the end and they shout as loud as they can.

"Lost, my dears?" Mrs. Pitcher's

voice sounds very near.

"Where are you? Are you so close?"

"It's a trick of the underground. But I am not so very far away."

"Help us, please," says Jane.

Mrs. Pitcher begins to call instructions to them. It's almost as if she can see where they are.

"Nearly there," she says after a little while and several twists and turns. "Did you find what you were looking for?"

"No!" shouts Charles at once. "No. It was all a waste of time."

Their next turn takes them to another dead end.

"It's not working, Mrs. Pitcher," calls Jane.

"Oh, dear. Try turning going back, then go the other way."

This has the same result.

"I don't understand this, "Mrs. Pitcher confesses. "And all this time and effort is wasted since you found nothing."

"That's right. Nothing," Charles echoes.

They turn and turn, but even with Mrs. Pitcher helping, they come up against another dead end every time.

"Never mind. We'll give it one more try," she says brightly. "Are you sure that none of you is bringing anything with you that you didn't have before?"

"Noth–" Charles begins.

"We found some jewels," calls Jane. "We found some jewels and I have them in the pocket of my dress."

"Good girl. True girl. Just two more turns, I think." And here's the familiar staircase up to the kitchen passage.

"I couldn't understand what was happening," Mrs. Pitcher says as she walks up the stairs with them. "I told you the right way, but it never worked. Never mind. No harm done. Here you are, now."

"How do you know?" asks Jane. "So many passages, and yet you can tell us which way to turn?"

"Oh, Mr. Darkling and I have been here for a long time, young Miss Jane. Yes. We've been here for a very long time." She seems lost in thought for a second.

"Would you like to see the jewels?"

"I think I would, yes please."

Jane unfolds the cloth and the jewels sparkle on the kitchen table. Mrs. Pitcher reaches out her hand and touches one or two of them with the tip of her finger, as if she remembers.

"We must tell the General," she says.

JUSTICE

Lak approaches our village. It's late afternoon by now. The sun is already touching the hilltops. Soon it will settle itself below the horizon, put on its nightcap, and snuggle up in bed for a well-deserved rest after a hard day's shining, while the moon does whatever it is the moon does. (Whatever it is, the moon seems to enjoy it a great deal, because sometimes she's still up and performing when the sun reappears. Like a singer who won't leave the stage.) Twilight and its half-world will soon slide across the valley, with all its uncertainties and possibilities. And then it will be night.

So Lak is keen to find a place to stay. Even without being too unkind you would have to admit that he is not in good condition. He is very tired. His clothes, already damaged in the wreck, are dusty. He is bruised and a cut is healing on his forehead. He looks the epitome of *the Stranger from a Strange Land*.

It's unfortunate for him that he is first noticed by a group of boys on the street, spinning out their time in the last minutes of the afternoon before they have to return home. Truth to tell, they're bored now, but refuse to go in without a fight. So Lak's appearance is a gift to them. He looks foreign and defenceless. They don't hesitate before shouting and throwing sticks and stones in his direction. He tries to protect his head and face with his arms, but there's nothing else he can do. The boys' shouting brings people out of their homes, and Lak hopes that some adult intervention will save him. But that's not what happens.

It's his further bad luck that a young woman is visiting her brother, the local blacksmith. She has come seeking refuge from the village on the south coast where she lives, because her husband was kidnapped by Moorish pirates. And as a far as she is concerned, that's what Lak appears to be. "Pirate!" she shouts. "Call the magistrate. Lock him up. Hang him!"

(Quite a lot is about to happen in a very short time now. Stand here, at the edge of the road opposite the inn, and you'll see it all without being noticed by anyone – they'll all be much too busy.)

The cries of "pirate" soon bring people flocking to see what is going on. The boys continue to pelt Lak with sticks and stones. Some of the adults begin to push him around – not actually beating him, but walking past and pushing him as if he were in their way, so that he begins to lose his balance and staggers back and forth along the path looking a little drunk – and it's a comical walk, if only he were doing it to entertain. It has that essential element of the clown's craft: the desperate attempt to retain some shred of dignity at all costs.

Robert, our actor, stands at the entrance to the inn's stables, watching. He wears hat and cloak, and feels as strong and powerful as he ever has. He has come upon the scene on his way to collect Jane from the General, as he promised this morning. He stays because he wants to see what happens. He thinks, *This is as good as bear-baiting*. He smiles to himself and takes a bite from an apple while he watches the fun.

But the fun is about to be ended. Our highwayman rides into town – not as a highwayman, of course, but just another young man on a horse. When he sees what is going on, he rides immediately to Lak's side, setting his horse between Lak and the children, and beating back the older tormentors with his rein.

And this is the moment when Jane and the twins arrive. They are on their way to the General, knowing he is in the inn. Seeing the commotion, they, too, want to find out what it's all about. Jane stops dead and can hardly speak.

"Lak?" she says.

Lak hasn't noticed her arrival, but turns at the sound of her voice. A grin spreads slowly across his face, which lights up so as to compete with the last of the sunlight, so happy is he to see her. He doesn't say anything at all, but she is running towards him, and he is holding out his arms, and they embrace.

This is confusing to the villagers, who feel bewildered and ashamed. But in a moment, something new will focus their attention.

The coach arrives, bearing the Justice and his escort. It's unusual for a coach to come to this village, but he is taking a shortcut. They draw up outside the inn and the Justice steps down, stretching his aching back and legs. There's total silence as everyone has a good look, wondering, *who can this Important Person be?* Our friend the highwayman is considering whether it's better to turn and run, or to stay and bluff it out in the hope that he isn't recognized. But then it's too late. He nearly gets away with it. He tips his hat to the Justice, who nods in return. He turns his horse and is beginning to walk away when the Captain of the Judge's escort believes that he recognizes, not the highwayman, but his horse.

"You! Stop now or my men will fire!" he shouts. And his men, quickly getting the idea, raise their muskets and level them at the highwayman. The Judge turns to take another look. "Is this the man who attempted a highway robbery, Captain?"

"I believe it is, sir."

"Why, then. We must arrest him and take him to the Assizes. We'll soon have him dancing at the end of our rope."

"My thoughts exactly, sir."

The highwayman looks around, and that's when Jane recognizes him, since she couldn't see him properly when he was on his horse with his face in silhouette against the sky. She doesn't want him hanged. She quite likes him – and has just seen him rescue her friend. But she can't think what to do. She looks around her desperately, searching for any kind of inspiration.

She catches sight of Robert, leaning nonchalantly against the doorpost, munching his apple. She knows immediately who he is and her heart leaps in fear. "Run!" her legs tell her, and she can't stop herself giving out a gasp of shock. The little noise she makes is enough in the complete silence that follows the clicking of the muskets. All attention is on her. She sees the faces turn towards her. She hears a voice shout, "You have the wrong man. There's your highwayman." She sees a familiar hand raised to point at Robert. She realizes the voice is hers, the hand her own.

Another voice rises above the immediate burble of gossip – a young woman with two young children. "That's right. He's the one. Robbed me of all I had. Take him! Hang him!"

The crowd take up the cry, as they always do when the song has such a stirring chorus. "Take him! Hang him!"

There's a moment of hesitation when the soldiers don't know what to do. Our highwayman remains calm. He knows the best thing for him is to do nothing. But Robert is not so cool. He turns and runs.

He doesn't get far. In a matter of minutes he is roped and loaded – daintily as a sack – onto the roof of the coach.

"My apologies, sir. I mistook you." The Captain magnanimously bows in our highwayman's direction. The highwayman bows in response.

"If I may be on my way?"

"Of course."

He mounts his horse again, kisses the tips of his fingers in Jane's direction, and gallops away – his back betrays not a whisper of the fear that still turns his insides to ice. (Truth to tell, he's shaking so much he can scarcely remain seated on his horse.) He doesn't breathe again until he is past the next town and can be sure that nobody is following.

(He has ridden out of our story, but – one last thing – you will be happy to know that he goes no more highway robbing. With the plunder he has saved he will buy a small farm in Lincolnshire, as far from his previous activities as possible. He will live a long and happy – though somewhat secluded – life, with only one further moment of fear. One day he will walk in the city of York and will see a familiar face – a man of roughly his own age and athletic build. The man will appear to recognize him, too. They will pass close to each other. The not-quite stranger will smile at our ex-highwayman.

"I had hoped to see you in less happy circumstances, sir. But you are welcome to your freedom." And he will pass on his way – the captain of the Judge's guard. Our sometime highwayman will not visit York again.)

Meanwhile, inside the inn, in the corner by the fire, James and the General sink deeper into clueless despair, totally oblivious of the excitements taking place only just outside the door. A clock chimes and startles the General into relative wakefulness again.

"Five o'clock, by Gad," he exclaims.

"I must fight off that young villain." As he speaks he is already standing, gathering his hat and stick and making his way outside with James following behind, half-awake and completely confused.

"Well done, young lady," the Judge congratulates Jane. "Had it not been for your quick eye, we should have allowed a villain to run free."

Jane curtsies as prettily as she knows how. "Thank you, sir," she says.

"Jane!" cries the General. "Take care. You're in terrible danger!"

Guessing his meaning, she giggles and points up at Robert, trussed and bundled across the roof of the carriage.

"Oh, excellent," says the General. He opens his mouth to ask how this came about, when he becomes aware of Lak, who still stands very close to Jane.

"A very dear friend," she says before he can speak. "I think we talked about him in London. And," she adds quickly, before the General can speak, "we shall talk some more; but not here." She dances over to him, her smile fairly lighting up the gathering dusk. "But, Uncle," she says. "I have something much more important to tell you. Something that will make you very happy." She holds her finger to her lips to shush the twins, who can scarcely control themselves and look likely to spoil her surprise. She stands on tiptoe to reach his ear, into which she whispers, "We have found the treasure. You are rich, uncle."

He can hardly believe his ears. She has to clap a hand to his mouth, or the entire countryside would know – which would not be sensible. He nods; and above her hand (which covers the lower part of his face), his eyes shine happily.

THE GREY LADY

Not much later, a small group of people walks up the driveway towards Nightride Priory, the General's house. Jane and the General, of course; Lak; the twins, who are determined to stay with Jane until they hear the whole story; and James, following because he doesn't know what else to do. He hasn't yet heard the Great Secret. The crowd has dispersed at last; the Judge, his carriage, and his soldiers have decided to stay the night in the inn; Robert, the failed highwayman, is locked in the cellars under guard – there has been so much hubbub that our friends have had no time to talk to each other. But now they are looking forward to sitting down together with a cup of tea, or of brandy.

They're in the courtyard at the front of the house now. Light is fading; stars beginning to show themselves. The General is already upon the steps. The front door opens, since Darkling has seen them coming. Jane turns to make sure that Lak is still with them. A shadow moves in the gathering darkness of the brick doorway to the stable yard, and is gone. Charlotte claps her hands to her mouth, so excited she can hardly speak. "The Grey Lady," she whispers. "I saw the Grey Lady."

"Nonsense, my dear. No such creature," gruffs the General.

But Lak is taking long strides across the courtyard towards the place where they might just, out of the corner of an eye, have seen a shadow flit out of sight.

"Elizabeth?" Jane hears him say, almost to himself, as if he has seen something and not believed the evidence of his eyes.

He disappears through the doorway into the stable yard. The General has marched ahead into the house. James, after a confused quivering, has finally made the decision to follow him. So only the three children stand on the steps, gazing at the place where Lak has gone and wondering whether to follow.

They hear a woman's quiet cry. A murmur of voices. The twins move forward, but Jane senses strongly that rushing in would be a mistake. She doesn't know what is happening around the corner, but she trusts Lak absolutely. She grabs the twins by the arm. "No. Wait. Give him time."

They start to shiver – partly from the cold of the falling night, and partly through a mix of trepidation and excitement. What will be coming back through that doorway?

"The General requests that you come inside." Darkling has returned, has whispered his way up behind them; but even this cannot disturb their concentration.

"Soon," says Jane.

And then, at last, two figures detach themselves from the shadow and walk together towards Jane and the twins. Jane finds she can scarcely breathe – and certainly she is unable to speak. Beside Lak is a smaller figure, shrouded in a grey cloak, with a hood concealing the face – the Grey Lady. They are now at the foot of the steps below Jane and the twins. Jane thinks that they are standing very close together – so close that she can't tell whether their hands are touching or not. They look at each other for support. Lak nods. The Grey Lady lifts her hands to the hood and throws it back to show her long, chestnut-brown hair, grey eyes, and a beautiful, worried face. Jane feels something catch in her stomach – or is it her heart? She can't breathe.

"Jane, this is your mother," says Lak. "Do you remember?"

The General is equally astonished and happy to see his sister after so many years, and is rendered practically speechless, his vocabulary being reduced to but three words: "splendid" and "more wine." James stands back, tactfully giving the family space to celebrate, but he watches with such a wide grin on his face that the top half of his head seems in danger of parting company with the lower and either falling to the floor or rising to the ceiling.

Dinner is a strange and loud affair, where everyone speaks in order to cover awkward silences – because, in the end, the meal is a collision of strangers. Jane's mother smiles a great deal but says very little. But she is clever enough at it, so that only afterwards do the other guests realize that she has said nothing of where she has been during the missing years when everyone supposed her dead.

But much later in the evening, when most of the house is in bed, a secret cat escapes from her story-bag after all.

Jane is just about to put out her candle when she hears furtive footsteps passing her door. Naturally she simply has to know who this is and where they walk so secretly. Stealthily she creeps along the landing to the top of the staircase. In the hall below, lit just enough by obliging moonlight to be recognizable, are Lak and her mother. They whisper seriously to each other. It looks as if they share some secret which they wish to hide from everyone else. At dinner they scarcely spoke to each other and sat well apart, so that Jane's suspicion of their closeness quite faded away. But now it seems she might have been right after all.

And then, all is certain.

They embrace.

Not a quick conspiratorial hug, but a long, tight, swaying cuddle.

Like two lovers who have been separated and found each other again.

"Lak!" Jane can't help but cry out. The couple turn suddenly and guiltily towards her. A quick whispered exchange and her mother rushes up the stairs. Jane wants to run, but she also wants to know what it is she has just seen. So she allows her mother to come to her and lead her back to her room.

"What is happening?" she hisses angrily. "What are you doing?"

Her mother paces around the room distractedly. She goes to the window, holds her hand to her forehead. She does not turn round. "Lak and I … we knew each other before."

THE YEW TREE

The yew tree carries a complicated mixture of meanings. It can live for a very long time – often more than two thousand years – and so signifies long life. For the ancient Celts – the Druids – the yew tree was a symbol of life, death, and resurrection, since a new tree can grow from a fallen branch. Some of the oldest yew trees grow in church graveyards – and were often growing before the church was built – and so they also have an air of death and sadness around them. Which is appropriate, because nearly every part of the tree is poisonous. On the other hand, extracts from the tree can be used as medicine, and so the yew can also heal. But then you will surely know that the yew-tree population of England (and Europe) was almost exterminated in medieval times because of the demand for its wood in the making of weapons – the long-bow, and the cross-bow, a weapon so deadly that in 1139 Pope Innocent II is said to have forbidden its use against Christians. Truly, the tree is a symbol of opposites: of life, and death.

An ancient yew tree grows in what was once the graveyard of the priory. Jane sits under it, her thoughts similarly in confusion. She doesn't know what she feels. She is overwhelmed. She is happy that her mother is here; but her mother is somebody she has never really known, and talking to her is awkward. She is happy that the General has the treasure and need no longer fear bankruptcy and the loss of his home. But she has grown fond of him and has begun to think of his home as her home, too. Now she fears she will have to leave it. She doesn't know whether she can handle her life being uprooted once more.

Last night. Her mother sits on Jane's bed and holds her hand, talking in a low voice.

"You ran away from me," whispers Jane. "You ran away from me."

"Not from you, my love. Not from you."

"But you hated India. You ran away and you didn't care about me – or Father."

"I didn't run away from you. I didn't want that. Your father was going to follow with you. To come here with you so we could all be together."

"But why did you hate India so much?"

Elizabeth is silent. She is hiding something. Something she doesn't want to say.

"What could make you hate the country so much that you left your own child, you own husband?"

Elizabeth grips her daughter's hand tighter. Another long silence. At last she speaks, her eyes fixed on the floor as if she might find some sort of absolution there.

"I didn't hate India."

"Then why?"

"I loved too much."

"I don't understand." Still her mother doesn't look at her.

"I loved everything about the country. And … not just the country …"

"Mother, I don't know what you're talking about. What are you trying to tell me?"

"I met somebody …" Another long pause. "And I loved him, too."

"Another man? Who was he?"

"And I couldn't stand it. I was young. I was confused. I didn't want to hurt your father. I still loved him. I really did. But I thought it would hurt him even more if I left him and lived with someone else in Amritsar. It was all too much for me. So I ran away from everything. By the time I stopped to think, I was already on a ship to England."

"And who was he? Do I know him? Does he still live in Amritsar?"

Her mother takes a deep breath. "It was Lak."

Her eyes fill with silent tears and she strokes Jane's hand up and down. "I wrote to your father. He promised to bring you to join me here. But he didn't come." She takes a deep shaky breath. "I have cried so much," she says at last.

"Feeling sorry for yourself. Your selfish self," Jane snaps.

"And for you. And for your father," her mother pleads. But she knows Jane is right.

Elizabeth wandered England, not daring to go to anyone she knew. Soon, she became used to her rootless existence and secretly spread the story that she had died. She found work as a governess with a family in Yorkshire and lived there for several years until the children grew too old for her. Not knowing where to go next, she wandered again, and found herself in the places of her childhood – the Priory where her brother lived; where they both had grown up. Still, she hid away and talked to no one.

"And one day I saw you. I knew straight away it was you. I dared not approach you. I was too frightened. So I sought out the shadows and watched you, and was happy to see you so grown up."

"The Grey Lady," Jane says.

"I suppose I was. I had forgotten the story, but yes. The Grey Lady."

"And what now?"

Her mother has no answer.

So Jane sits under the tree and doesn't know what to think. She is very happy that she has her mother; she is very happy that Lak has come back into her life, because in that short time in London he became a sort of father-substitute for her. But Lak was the reason her mother left her when she was a baby – and left her father. So she should really be hating him; hating both of them. But she can't.

A hand grasps her shoulder. She shrieks and leaps up. The General is almost as surprised as she and jumps backwards at the suddenness of her reaction. There's a moment of stillness and they both burst out laughing.

"I'm sorry, my dear. I had no intention of startling you so."

Much to his surprise, she hugs him. He pats her back, then pushes her gently away.

"I have something to say, my dear. I think it's better said just between the two of us. Shall we sit?"

He settles himself beside her on the ruined wall. "I've always loved this tree, too," he says. "It will have seen so much. So many lives living out their little worries and great passions under these branches. Puts it all in perspective." The General is not normally given to such depth of thought, and pauses for a moment, having surprised himself. He turns to face Jane.

"So this is the 'friend' that the Colonel was so interested in?"

Jane nods, fearing what is coming next.

"The one who caused you to act – what shall I say? – who caused you to act against your country?"

"Not really *my* country, Uncle."

"Ah, yes. Therein lies our little problem, does it not?"

Jane turns to look at him. "What do you mean?"

The General takes her hand in his and pats it as he speaks. "I have ... I have spent my whole life in the service of my country, Jane. This country. My home." He looks around, soaking up the landscape – his landscape. "Many times I've lain awake in faraway lands and dreamt of home. This ..." he gestures to include the yew tree, the meadow, the house behind him, "... has always been the reason I fought so long and so hard in so many places. Horrible places, sometimes. Beautiful places, too – but they were not England." He gazes intently at her. "Do you understand me, my dear?"

She nods. She guesses what he is about to say and hopes with all her heart that she is wrong.

"I will be brief. Never was one to beat about the bush. Never helps. Last night I sent post-haste to London to our friend the Colonel – you remember?" Jane nods, tears already welling in her eyes. "It's a matter of honour. I can do no other. I'm sorry, my dear." He pats her hand once more before he stands. "The Colonel's men will be here by evening. I suspect that even if your friend were to run now, it would be too late. They would surely catch him." And he walks away.

PART FOUR

FUGITIVE

I suppose I shouldn't be surprised, Jane reflects later, *that Mother panics.* It was panic that took her from India and her own daughter all those years ago. She has been no help in protecting Lak. When Jane tells her what the General has done, she really, actually, literally does rush around in circles in the room, flapping her hands helplessly, and crying, "What shall we do? What shall we do? Oh, Jane, what shall we do?" *She looks like a mechanical toy,* Jane thinks. *Like a figure set to run in a circle as the clock strikes twelve.*

But she does not laugh, and she does not scream and shout in frustration. She does not do these things because she has a

Plan. It's so obvious that she doesn't even think of herself as clever. And it's obvious, too, that she can tell nobody, because it's too difficult to know who she can trust. Lak must not flee, but disappear.

She leaves her mother turning on her invisible merry-go-round and finds Lak strolling in the orchard, enjoying the peace and freedom from worry that he has found in the few hours that he has been in this beautiful, remote place.

He does not panic. Nor does he throw up his hands and turn in circles. Quietly, and stealthily, he follows Jane through the kitchen courtyard, along the dusty corridors to Mrs. Pitcher's private domain, where she keeps the key that unlocks the Graven Owl.

The room is empty. Through the glass in the door you can see an empty cup on the little table. Mrs. Pitcher is somewhere else, probably complaining to Darkling about the extra work she has to do with all these guests. There haven't been so many people in the house since the General and his sister were children. Jane's heart thumps. She needs to remain calm and move quickly before Mrs.

Pitcher returns. She pushes Lak around a corner and whispers to him to keep out of the way. Then she tiptoes as quietly as she can up to the door of Mrs. Pitcher's room and turns the handle. She feels herself becoming a little breathless as she pushes the door, slowly, as slowly as she can, and steps into the room. She knows where the key is, because she secretly watched when Mrs. Pitcher opened the door for her with the twins. She goes straight to the little drawer at the bottom of the cupboard. Still no sound in the corridor outside. The drawer sticks. It won't open. It's locked. She grits her teeth and wiggles the drawer in silent frustration – and it comes loose. She gasps in excitement and relief. Slowly, slowly she opens the drawer. And there's the key. She grabs it and runs from the room, almost giggling with triumph. She should have known better than to think she'd get away undiscovered.

"'More haste, less speed' is the saying, as I believe." It's the sound of dried leaves blowing over abandoned courtyards; of dust falling from crumbling stone. Yet Darkling has never seemed so solid.

"I ... I was ..."

"... seeking to conceal your Indian friend in the labyrinth ..."

"Yes."

"An excellent idea. But you do place me in an extremely tricky situation, since I know the General feels it his duty to dispatch your friend to London. What am I to do?"

He moves slowly as he whispers, and it is only when his voice has faded into silence that Jane realizes that Darkling has placed himself inside Mrs. Pitcher's room.

"Lak!" she shouts. She slams the door shut on Darkling and turns the key in the lock. Through the glass of the door, she sees what might be the ghost of a smile on his face, though smeared by the distortion of the thick panes. She takes a lantern from a nearby dresser, runs with Lak to the Graven Owl, unlocks the gates, opens the door, and pushes him into the darkness of the labyrinth.

"Don't go too far, or you might never get out again," she whispers to him. Then she locks the gates again and runs to the kitchen courtyard.

She emerges onto the gravel in front of the house to see a company of soldiers galloping up the drive, terrible in their haste and self-importance. Quickly she ducks back through the gateway, returns to the kitchen passages, and winds her way through the inside of the house, keeping to the servants' stairs and corridors, which are always separate and hidden from the family rooms, until she is in the drawing room where she had left her mother.

Already she can hear a great bustle downstairs. Darkling is not there to open the door, of course, so in the end the General has gone himself to answer the thundering of military fist on wood. It has not put him in the best of tempers, and he is not intimidated by soldiers – particularly since it was he who summoned them here. Jane can't hear the words, but it's clear that a disagreement in staccato form is taking place below.

"He's safe," she whispers quickly to her mother. "Be still, now."

"But where is he? How can he be safe?"

"You can honestly tell them that you don't know where he is." She stares hard at her mother, who drops her gaze. "Yes," she says.

Suddenly the soldiers are in the room, followed by Mrs. Pitcher, who looks daggers at them but knows there's nothing she can do. The officer bows low. "Forgive me, ladies," he says. "It is our duty to be thorough in our search."

Of course, they find nothing, and march into the next room, still followed closely by Mrs. Pitcher.

Night falls, candles are lit, and still the soldiers tramp around the house, opening doors to cupboards and rooms, insisting that keys be found to locks that have not been turned for generations. Jane can't help herself, though she knows it's the wrong thing to do, and she follows them, too, pretending to admire their uniforms and their manly strength (though her real thoughts are much more "what self-satisfied fools"). She can feel her throat tighten and her breathing quicken as they enter the depths of the kitchen passages. They find Darkling and release him, to his pretended gratitude (a strange sight in itself) and Mrs. Pitcher's amazement in finding him in her room. They bring bright lanterns to illuminate the dusty corners of hidden passages. At one time, they turn a familiar corner, and Jane nearly cries out. But they don't find the Graven Owl. "Because the Graven Owl does not wish to be found," Mrs. Pitcher says later, something which Jane never quite forgets.

At last they are gone. The General offers the stables for the night, but these soldiers are used to London, and beds, so they make themselves unpopular in the inn – though their money is welcome, their manners are not. They are probably extra grumpy because first they have to search the woods and fields around the village. It's not easy at night, and actually somewhat futile, but they have to do their duty.

As soon as she sees the soldiers' lanterns leave the Priory grounds, Jane disappears once more into the hidden corridors to unlock the Graven Owl and release Lak from the labyrinth. He is dusty, tired, and very glad to come out. But Jane won't allow him to rest. "You have to go. You must not stay here. The General is angry. You are in great danger. If he finds you, he will give you to the soldiers."

"Elizabeth …" he croaks with his dusty throat. Jane thinks quickly.

"We will meet you in Bath. Go." She pushes him out into the night.

The General is with her mother when she returns to the dining room.

"Odd they couldn't find him," he says, crisply.

"Perhaps he ran away," says Jane's mother.

"You warned him, of course," the General says to Jane. She doesn't know how to answer. Her brain spins uselessly, unable to engage a single thought. Whatever she says will be a lie or a betrayal or, at the very least, a great disobedience. She seizes on that most potent of weapons available to women in the nineteenth century. She faints.

THE UNWISE ROAD

Lak uses the night to walk as far as he can in what he hopes is the direction the soldiers will not expect – towards London, not away. It's a good plan. Unfortunately the captain of the soldiers has had a better one. He left two of his men to watch the Priory, just in case the fugitive should still be there, and not already on the road. The men have dark cloaks covering their uniform, so even if they should be seen, they will not be recognized for what they are. And they are angry, because they resent that they are kept from the warmth of the inn and the society of their brothers in arms, so they intend to make sure that their suffering is justified. If any living creature at all should come from the house, whether small as a mouse or big as a horse, they are determined that they will see it.

And so Lak, being certainly bigger than a mouse, though not as large as a horse, has little chance of escape, and is captured with a shout of triumph that even Jane, also known as Suri, can hear in her supposed faint in her bedroom. She turns over in bed and curls up very small. What can she do now?

The decision is made for her. She comes down to breakfast to find the General and his sister in the middle of a furious argument. The captain of the soldiers has been to the house early to thank the General for his help and inform him that they have now caught the spy and are departing for London. That was two hours ago. Elizabeth has heard the news and is not pleased with her brother.

"George, you are nothing but a stuffed prig. How can you think it right to put your so-called duty before the well-being of your family?"

The General is contemptuous. "Stuffed prig?" he echoes.

"Jane has saved your bacon; saved your house, and yet you feel it right to betray our friend."

"Ah … and there's the rub, is it not, dear sister? Jane's friend being the very same 'friend' with whom you betrayed her father."

"To give him up to the soldiers; to give him up to his death. You … you …

you Judas!"

She has no more words, but sweeps from the room, taking Jane by the arm as she passes.

"Come, Jane, we will stay here no longer."

And she is true to her word. Within little more than half an hour, she has had the pony and trap prepared, and their small amount of baggage loaded. "Take everything, Jane," she says. "We shall not be returning." By mid-morning they are clip-clopping out through the Priory gates and on their way to catch the stagecoach to London.

THE RIGHT SCHOOL

At this time about 850,000 people live in London. By the time Jane becomes an old lady (while the yet-to-be-born Victoria is still Queen) the number will have grown to four million. The city and the country around it are about to go through the most explosive time of growth in its two-thousand-year history, and it needs paying for. Now, not yet at the end of a long war against Napoleon, the nation is poor, and there are harsh times ahead. There is revolution in the air for England, too, although not in such a dramatic way as across the Channel in France.

To distract and pacify the rebels at home, the ruling powers take the search for wealth into other countries; for example, they will take over the East India Company's activities in India and occupy the entire sub-continent in the name, not of the Company, but of England. In this way, the riches of India can be plundered and brought home, just as the riches of Africa have been; and those of anywhere else that the legitimized, nationalized pirates of England are able to get a foothold. Because England needs the money. This process of robbery is dignified and disguised with the stirring label, *Empire*.

This is what the Colonel is about in capturing and subduing Lak and his friends. This is why it matters so much, and why Lak cannot be allowed to escape.

Lak is brought to London and taken straight to the Colonel, who greets him politely. The appearance of a warm welcome is slightly undermined by the two burly, out-of-uniform soldiers who bring him in and who stand either side of him as the Colonel invites him to sit.

"I'm so pleased you were able to come. I've heard so much about you," says the Colonel. Lak stares back at him in silence.

Perhaps there's no need to drag out the unpleasant details of that evening. Lak is beaten. He still refuses to speak, and is eventually removed to a small, dark, stone chamber in the depths of Newgate prison, where (for all he knows) he will be left to rot. And, under normal circumstances, that would be the end of him. He is a spy, and a danger to the interests of

Britain. He will be hanged, or shot, depending on the whim of Colonel Jenkins, and this will happen whether he changes his mind and tries to save his skin by betraying his friends, or whether he nobly holds his tongue to the end.

To men like Jenkins, England is everything, and anyone who does not think in precisely the same way is not a true human being. In fact, if you did not go to the same school as Jenkins, or one very like it, you cannot truly be considered a member of the human race, and you are likely to be thrown off like a soiled glove at the first sign of disloyalty to the ruling class. God is an Englishman – and further, an Englishman who went to the right school.

Hardfist did not go to the right school. Nor did most of the people in his world. Had Robert, the poor (in every sense of the word) actor and short-lived highwayman, gone to school at Eton instead of nearly not at all, he might have ended his life in luxury and idleness instead of choking at the end of a rope after the assizes at Exeter.

Hardfist has just heard of Robert's

last moments, and for a few brief seconds he is sad. But then he thinks, like most of those who get caught, Robert died because his stupidity was greater than his villainy – *and,* he thinks, *I have problems of my own.*

He has heard that Elizabeth has reappeared. So Jane's grandmother now has no claim at all over Jane, and Hardfist has no hope of any more money from her – although it won't stop him trying. He is more than slightly desperate, and owes money everywhere – for rent, for food, for clothes, and – worse – to people who don't give second chances when payment is overdue. So run his thoughts, and then he hears the sound of several determined boots on the stair.

Over the centuries there have been many reasons why particular people would want to run or hide – people of the wrong religion, or nation, or profession. And old houses, with many secrets, grow to be kind to some of these people. So in Hardfist's lodgings, the attic floors are not blocked at the point that corresponds to each street door, but continue unbroken through the whole building. Hardfist leaves his rooms through a hidden exit and runs across three neighbouring houses before emerging on the street a hundred feet from his own front door. He does not wait to see if he is followed.

He walks to Cavendish Square. He knows that there is no hope for him here, but he is so desperate that he will try anything to gain a few guineas – or pennies – so that he can delay the moment that he now feels is inevitable, when he will be found floating face-down in the Thames.

He knocks at Jane's grandmother's door, and to his surprise is shown up to the drawing room. Where he is made to wait for the best part of half an hour before the grandmother appears.

"Hardfist. You have something for me?"

Hardfist coughs – a nervous reaction.

"The girl's mother …"

"My daughter."

"Quite so. Has appeared, it seems."

"Yes. I have heard."

"This of course makes it difficult …"

"I have no interest in difficulties. What can you do?"

Hardfist tries his best to appear suave

and confident.

"With the help of some of my … associates, I may be able to restore the girl to your influence."

She reaches out her hand. He is surprised to see a guinea coin in her fingers. He takes it. She sweeps away towards the door.

"There will be more if you succeed."

A few seconds later he finds himself on the street once more. As he hurries away towards Oxford Street, he does not see Jane and her mother drive up to the house.

It was Jane's idea. Elizabeth has spent most of her life avoiding her mother and has no wish to see her now. But Jane has remembered Hardfist. It seems like a very long time ago that she feared him. She has seen a great deal more of English people and of London since then, and now remembers him mostly for the atmosphere of seediness and bad luck that surrounds him. He is just the man they need – the man to haunt the city's dungeons and find Lak, she thinks. She doesn't know where to find Hardfist, so, unpleasant though it is, she will have to ask her grandmother.

It is Jane who is first up the steps. It is Jane who rings the bell. And it is Jane who laughs with relief when the door is timidly opened by Daisy Sweetly (you remember her, the aptly named maid of all work). Jane suddenly thinks that she won't have to speak to her grandmother. Surely the servants will know. But Daisy doesn't know. She says she will talk to Jimmy Pocket. She's sure he has sometimes been sent with messages for Mr. Hardfist. Jane and Elizabeth wait uncomfortably in the entrance hall while Daisy runs in search of Jimmy. They are both nervous, hoping that Grandmother will not choose this moment to sally forth from her chamber. They are unlucky.

"Poker! Poker, who's at the door?" A few seconds pause. A frantic jangling of the hand bell that Grandmother always keeps by her, and now largely ignored by the company of servants. (It's how they keep sane, for surely the constant ringing would make their heads burst if they were to pay any attention to it. So, just as people who live by a road soon cease to hear the traffic, Grandmother's servants no longer hear her furious bell.)

"Oh! Why do we have servants if we must do all the work ourselves?" With this exasperated cry and a pointed rustle of skirts, Grandmother appears at the top of the stairs. She is struck momentarily mute by the sight of her visitors. But only momentarily.

"Poker! Sweetly! Pocket! Somebody! Pocket, I say. Poker! Take her! Seize her! She shall not leave this house!"

To Jane it seems almost as if Grandmother's face has disappeared, and her grey hair become a thundercloud such as clings to the top of a mountain, sparking with lightning bolts and shining with rain. She giggles at the image, which does not calm the older woman.

At this moment, Jimmy Pocket appears. And Jane prepares to run.

"Pocket!" the grandmother shouts. "Seize the girl. Throw the mother out. I have no daughter! Bring the girl to me!"

It's all too much for Jimmy, who is quite unable to follow the torrent of instruction, so ignores it altogether. He pushes a folded piece of paper into Jane's hand as Elizabeth is already opening the front door – keen to be away as soon as she can. "Can you read?" he whispers to Jane. She nods. "Hardfist's lodgings," he says, and closes the door behind them.

Hardfist is a suspicious individual – he both arouses suspicion in others and looks on the world with suspicion. But at this moment, he appears to be in a situation where he cannot lose. If he succeeds in what Jane and her mother are asking, then they will reward him handsomely (and he is well aware of the extent of Jane's fortune). If, on the other hand, he should fail, then he is sure that he will find a way to deliver the girl to her grandmother and will be duly rewarded by her.

"Why do you suppose I can find this man of yours? I promise you I have no special connection to the Colonel."

"We are trusting to your deep knowledge of this city, to which we are almost strangers, Mr. Hardfist," says Elizabeth. "I am sure you realize that it would be greatly rewarding for all of us here, in different ways, if you were able to find and secure the release of our friend."

Elizabeth is a very attractive woman, and Hardfist eats up her flattery as a mouse gobbles the cheese in a trap. (Let's hope the results are less fatal for him than for the mouse.) Be that as it may, though he has given up his freedom to her, he is giving nothing else away. "I will make some enquiries. And I shall need some funds for expenses. Where can I find you?" They name the inn where they are staying, Elizabeth lays a number of coins on the table, and soon they stand (with some relief) in the relative safety of Fleet Street.

NEWGATE

Hardfist has no intention of trying to speak to the Colonel directly. More and more, Hardfist is becoming a creature of darkness, hidden corners, dungeons, and night. He is happiest in the rookeries, where we have previously followed him – the slums filled with people who dream of hope as you and I dream of a sudden fortune, or a perfect house. Hope is a thing long ago lost – or never possessed. His mean, crumbling lodgings, deep in a forgotten courtyard of a forgotten inn of court are the closest he comes to respectability, and – having reconciled himself to this – he is happy in his way.

So his search for Lak will begin at the end, at a place which is indeed the end for many who enter its walls, and is feared by everyone who walks into it – or even just passes by. Newgate prison. Hardfist doesn't know whether Lak is in Newgate, but there's a good chance that, even if he isn't, somebody there will know where he is.

He will visit a friend, who has a friend called John Langley. If you were of an age to remember (but you look far too young), the names of John Langley and the man he works for, William Brunskill, would turn the blood to ice in your veins, and you would likely still be shivering tomorrow. Because William Brunskill is England's chief Hangman, and Langley his assistant. During his time as Hangman, Brunskill executes 537 men and women, and when he retires, John Langley will continue his work.

Assistant Hangman Langley is in his early forties. He's not somebody whose company you'd seek out over a mug of beer, but somehow he has found a wife and has three children with her. She is said to be an odd woman – very fond of talking, and proud of her husband, which some of her neighbours find somewhat chilling. The following evening (a Tuesday) Hardfist is brought to their home by his friend and spends a pleasant hour in the armchair by the fire. Have you ever met somebody for the first time, and felt straight away that you've always been friends? So it is with Hardfist in the Langley home.

Because of this, Langley promises

that he will find out if Lak is in Newgate, and if he is not, where he might be. He agrees that – if Lak is indeed in the prison – it might be arranged that someone could visit. He agrees to this, not just because of Elizabeth's guineas, but because he feels he has a new friend in Hardfist.

Hardfist is hoping that he will not have to go to Newgate himself. He owes too much money to too many people, and he is frightened by the thought that once he enters, he might never come out again.

We must all wait a few days while Langley asks around. On Thursday morning, he, too, is given a fright. As he turns the corner into Newgate Street, he notices a gentleman crossing the road. The gentleman wears an expensive cloak, and a hat shadows his face. Langley pays him no more attention, and is surprised to find himself knocked off balance, as if by accident, so that he falls against the prison wall.

"Mr. Langley," says the gentleman. "If you wish to avoid dancing at the end of one of your own ropes, I suggest you do not concern yourself with India."

But the warning is too late. Only a

few minutes later, one of the warders – a man he's known since childhood – whispers that his Indian is in one of the punishment cells. No visitors allowed.

Langley sends a boy to Hardfist with a message to call at his home in the evening where he tells him the news. Hardfist reveals the tips of his teeth. He is happy. He leans forward so that nobody else can hear.

"The interested parties are not financially embarrassed," he says in a low voice. "Would my friend know of someone who might be inclined to … er … slacken a few chains?"

Langley has been unsettled by the behatted gentleman, and perhaps reacts with less restraint than he might otherwise have done. As it is, he leaps to his feet, grabs Hardfist by the collar, and shoves him abruptly out of the room and the house so that he sprawls on the rain-soaked street outside, where his hand – put out to break his fall – sinks deep into a pile of horse-manure.

"I'll make believe we never met, Mr. Hardfist. Think yourself lucky." The door slams behind him.

From which Hardfist understands that Langley's answer is "no." He doesn't want a bribe. He could just have said …

SOLDIER, SOLDIER

Elizabeth is startlingly decisive when she hears what happened, in complete contrast to the panic she previously exhibited.

"I shall need pen and paper, a military seal of some sort, sealing wax, and the uniform of a lieutenant in the Rifles. I shall also need a pistol. You can bring me these by noon tomorrow?" She pushes several coins across the table where they sit in the corner of the inn. Hardfist collects them without a word. He gives no hint that this is the most money he has held in his hand for many years. Nor does he give any sign that he finds her requests in any way strange. He nods. "Until noon tomorrow. Good day, ladies."

However hard she tries, Jane gets nothing from her mother – no explanation of why she has asked for this strange collection of objects, or what she intends to do with them. She is torn between frustration and admiration. Up to this moment she has been (honestly) disappointed in her mother, who has seemed to do nothing. She has allowed every decision to be made for her and has followed Jane in everything. And now suddenly she has come over all commanding and decisive. And secretive. The twenty-four hours until the following noon are long for Jane (and for Elizabeth, too – but only she knows that).

Hardfist arrives carrying a bundle wrapped in black cloth. He is clearly very nervous, and is relieved when Elizabeth takes him into their upstairs chamber.

"Thank you," she says, as Jane unwraps the bundle. He has brought everything. Elizabeth sits down at once and begins to write a letter. And Jane suddenly realizes what her plan must be.

"No. You can't do this."

"Why not?" Elizabeth continues to write.

"They'll catch you. They'll lock you up, and then I'll be all alone again."

"And if they don't catch me, we shall all be together. There ..." She sprinkles some fine sand over the ink to dry it, shakes the sand off, and folds the paper. "You have the seal? Good. Now please leave me. I shall join you at the street corner before the inn."

The streets are busy and noisy. At first Jane tries to make polite conversation with Hardfist, but he can't hear her light voice above the rattling and clopping of carts, barrows, and horses. Everyone seems to be shouting, and because there's so much noise, everyone shouts louder. So they stand side by side and watch the people and the traffic flowing past.

A girl slightly younger than Jane stands on the other side of the road, selling flowers. Anyone can see that she's very poor. Her dress is torn and she wears a faded shawl draped over her shoulders. A young soldier walks up and says something to her that makes her smile and look shyly away. The soldier says something else, and the girl looks straight at Jane. Why? Now they're walking towards her, the soldier and the flower girl.

The soldier speaks to Jane, but she can't hear. He leans closer to speak in her ear. She forces herself not to shy away. "Change clothes with the girl," says the soldier. Jane leans back to say "What!?" and only then gets a good look at the soldier's face. It's her mother.

Before she can react, she is turned

around and pushed through the archway into the inn courtyard.

"Take the girl to your room and change clothes with her," says the soldier languidly. "You can both keep your new clothes. Here's a shilling for a posy, girl." He gives the flower girl a coin (a great deal of money, and much more than the flowers are worth) and pushes them both away. "Quick as you can."

The next hour is probably the closest that Elizabeth and Jane come to an unnaturally early death – and that's including the terrified weeks they will spend during what the British call the Indian Mutiny, more than forty years later.

They take a (rather battered) hackney carriage to the Old Bailey and stop outside the great grey grim granite of Newgate Prison. Hardfist doesn't want to know what their plan is, and refuses to come with them, so the soldier and the flower girl travel alone.

The carriage stops. Nobody moves.

"Changing our minds, are we?" the driver calls back to them. "Most people do."

They each take a deep breath and

climb down. The soldier gives a shilling to the driver. "Wait for us, please. Across the road," he says. Later the driver will report that he seemed very young, and had a surprisingly light voice.

The flower girl stands on the corner where the Old Bailey meets Newgate Street and tries to sell her few pitiful posies. The soldier takes a paper from his pocket and knocks on the doors of the prison. The driver watches him go in before he moves his carriage across the road to wait – for a while at least.

Elizabeth feels the prison door shut behind her and feels that her life is ending. But she must be the soldier or she has no chance.

"I must see the Governor," she says in her soft deep voice. The very fact that she does not shout or bark instructions at the porter makes him treat her with respect. He leads her along a dark corridor and up a lighter staircase. At each corner a door is unlocked, and locked again behind them once they are through. It is as Hardfist has said. There have been escapes from Newgate in the distant past, but now without influence, bribery, or deceit, there is no release except death, or the end of a sentence.

"How can I help you, lieutenant?"

The Governor is a rotund, red-faced man of fifty, who looks at first sight as if he might be jolly company. But there is a flintiness in his eye and a sharpness around the nose. He is the right man for the job.

"I come from Colonel Jenkins …"

"Ah, yes. Jenkins. He is well?"

"I left him well, thank you, sir."

"And?"

"He writes …" She holds out the sealed letter to him. "… to ask that you release the Punjabi prisoner to my care so that I can deliver him to the Colonel for further interrogation."

The Governor takes the letter, breaks open the seal, and reads. Elizabeth's heart threatens to break free and fly across the room. She coughs to conceal the rising of fear in her throat. At last the Governor lays the letter on his desk.

"Very well." He pulls the bell-rope. "Johnson here will take you to the prisoner."

The door opens and a uniformed prison guard stands in the doorway.

"Thank you, sir."

"It's strange that he should change his mind."

Elizabeth is shaking and hopes it doesn't show. "Sir?"

"I happened to see the Colonel last afternoon, and he seemed clear that he would leave the prisoner here to rot – that was his phrase."

Elizabeth smiles wanly. "Operational necessity, sir. The situation has changed."

"Of course. Good day to you, Lieutenant. And my compliments to the Colonel."

"Thank you, sir."

The solitary punishment cells in Newgate are the furthest from the street door, across two courtyards at the very rear of the prison. There are many doors and barred gates to unlock, walk through, and lock once more before they reach the corridor of the cells.

Johnson pauses at the last door. "If you wouldn't mind, sir, just lift your arms."

"What? Why?"

"I just need to be sure you have no hidden weapons or little tools to pass to the prisoner, sir." He smiles. "It's a rule, sir. We have to stick to the rules."

Now, if the lieutenant that Johnson sees before him were to submit to this frisking, however perfunctory, he'd have quite a different idea of the lieutenant afterwards. Somehow this has to be prevented. The lieutenant laughs softly. "Oh, come, man. You cannot think that the personal aide of Colonel Jenkins could possibly wish to pass a weapon to the prisoner."

Johnson laughs, too. "A foolish idea, indeed, sir."

Elizabeth breathes a little more freely.

"Nevertheless. Rules is rules, sir. If you'll permit." Johnson comes closer, his hands outstretched.

Elizabeth thinks as fast as she can. Time slows, as it often does at times of great stress. Johnson's pace towards her separates into its several parts. He transfers his weight to his right foot. *I can't let him touch me.* He lifts his left foot. *What can I do?* His left foot travels towards her. *I could bribe him.* He shifts his weight ready to transfer it to the left foot once it is safely on the floor. *But that would give me away, too. I could fight him.* The left foot touches the flagstone. *No. I couldn't fight him.* The right foot – now behind – begins to lift from the floor. *I could try to seduce him. He'll know I'm a woman, and some say I'm quite attractive ...* The right foot travels through the air to meet its companion, the left, which waits steadfastly for its lifelong companion. *I must play out the game. I must intimidate him.* The right foot steadies itself on the flagstone and Johnson stands close enough to touch her.

She steps back a pace.

"I regret that the rule must be broken." There's a hard edge to her voice, low though she speaks. "You may not presume to manhandle an officer of His Majesty's Rifles. I warn you. It will go badly for you if you lay your hands on me."

He hesitates. "I will speak on your behalf should it ever be necessary." She reaches out and claps him hard on the shoulder. "But if you don't speak of this moment, then neither shall I. Now quickly, deliver the prisoner to me and we shall go our separate ways."

She stares firmly into his eyes. *What will he do?* The firm gaze of duty wavers just a little. She seizes her advantage. "Come now." She twirls her hand in the air to show him what to do. "Turn around and let's continue."

Johnson turns. He has been on duty since shortly after midnight, and he honestly isn't enjoying the work as much as he used to when he was younger. As long as no prisoner escapes, he considers his duty done. He has worked his way up in this prison from the most junior guard to the trusted right hand of the Governor himself. It has taken him twenty-five years, and he knows that the rules are not always the most important thing. Still, a small voice rings in his head as he unlocks the door. "Rules are there to protect us, young Johnson, not to confine us," something drummed into them again and again when they were young recruits, all that time ago. Good old Hatherstone. Little and loud. Dead now, poor chap. Sadly, he should have listened to the little voice.

Elizabeth enjoys the sound of the turning lock so much that, without thinking, she closes her eyes. She snaps them open before Johnson can see.

One more lock to go. And there he is.

Lak looks up to see the young officer in the dark uniform of the Rifle Regiment (it has been part of his work to learn the uniforms and insignia). He sighs but doesn't move from his place on the floor in the corner of the cell. A great depression has lain over him these last days. He knows that he will die here, and he is ready. They cannot touch him any longer. He has withdrawn to somewhere deep inside himself, and his days are spent in the cool hills and hot plains of his childhood.

"You won't get much out of him, sir," Johnson chuckles.

"Help me get him up," Elizabeth snaps.

It's a long, long walk back to the front gate of the prison. Approach a door, shout your name, unlock the door, drag the prisoner through. Lock behind you. On to the next. At last the opening door is the one that leads onto the street.

"There you are, sir. Good day to you, now."

"Thank you, Johnson. My compliments to the Governor, and … buy the wife some flowers …" Elizabeth drops a crown into Johnson's hand. He smiles his surprised thanks. And the prison gate shuts behind him.

It's a grim, grey day, but brighter outdoors than in the prison corridors, and now she can see Lak's face for the first time, bruised and swollen. She gasps and shakes away the tears that prickle her eyes. He pays no attention. He is not looking at her. Not looking at anything, really, just mechanically moving as she pulls him along. The shell is here, but the man is gone.

TRAFFIC

The soldier lifts his fingers to his mouth and gives out a great loud whistle. Jane looks round from her corner and laughs. She had no idea her mother could do that. The waiting carriage driver is startled out of his sleep, where he has been dreaming of a great joint of roast beef in his own little home, with his little wife to cook it for him (he is not married and lives above a stables), and brings the carriage across the road to meet the soldier and his prisoner.

The flower girl – Jane – begins to walk rapidly towards them. There's a commotion further along Snow Hill where it approaches Newgate Street. Two or three men on horseback are forcing their way through the traffic. She can't see clearly enough, but it doesn't look good. She breaks into a run. "Quick! They're coming!"

Elizabeth doesn't stop to ask who it is that's coming, but it still takes an age to get Lak aboard the carriage. The door of the prison opens behind them, and two warders come out into the street. Luckily it's quite crowded now, and the carriage doesn't stand out as it did when they arrived. Elizabeth guesses that the Governor mistrusted her and sent to ask Colonel Jenkins if he really had asked for the prisoner to be sent to him.

"Across the bridge. Quick as you can," Elizabeth shouts. Her shout is a woman's and the driver hesitates, confused.

"A guinea for you!" yells Jane. Since that's as much as he earns in a month, it does the trick. They are away as fast as they can go (considering the London traffic) across Blackfriars bridge. Behind them, like a storm approaching across a summer field, they can see the horsemen fighting their way through the traffic. London is an ancient city. Many things have changed in its two thousand years, but the terrible traffic is not one of them. If you have ever tried to hurry through London's streets, you'll know how futile the effort is, and so it has always been. This is a slow-motion chase, but it's no less serious for that. At last they are across the bridge and into the huddle of little streets south of the river. Jane and

Elizabeth could jump down and run. It would be easy for them to disappear completely. But Lak can scarcely walk, and still seems unaware of what is happening to him. They have no choice but to trust their driver.

"We are being followed and must not be found," Elizabeth says. Luckily for them, the driver is getting into the spirit of the day and beginning to enjoy it. He has also begun to think that if he is caught helping an escape, then he is in big trouble, too. He whips his horse enthusiastically and their speed increases to a breath-taking five miles an hour, carving a way through the crowded little street like Moses through the Red Sea.

The horsemen have not yet appeared in the street behind them when they turn suddenly left, into a mews at the end of which are several stables.

"You go into the loft," he says. "I'll leave you here." He sees their hesitation. "You'll just have to trust me, won't you, ladies?"

And soon he has gone with his guinea, and they have dragged Lak up the ladder into the stables' hay loft.

There's no denying it. Whatever you think of Hardfist, he doesn't give up easily. At this very moment he is back in Cavendish Square, a spring in his step, since he smells money coming his way. His life is in such a state that he doesn't care what people think of him any more, as long as he can persuade a few coins from them. Or preferably a great number of coins. He rings the bell and is shortly in the Presence. Grandmother has absolutely no confidence or trust in him, but is always willing to listen, just in case.

"Yes, Mr. Hardfist?"

"I know where your granddaughter is to be found."

"Excellent. She has been here, but I was unable to detain her. So where is she now?"

"I can bring her to you ... but there will be expenses ..."

Grandmother rings the servants' bell and waits unusually calmly, and without saying a word, until the butler appears. "Poker, bring the captain upstairs."

Hardfist guesses what has happened. "Oh, gracious, is that the time? I will return, Madam, be assured." But it's too late. All at once the room seems full of soldiers. Colonel Jenkins's real aide and three infantrymen have called at the house in search of Jane, and since she is not there, they are happy to take Hardfist away with them to the Colonel instead. Ever optimistic (and in another triumphant display of hope over experience), Hardfist wonders if he might be able to persuade the Colonel to pay for information.

The fugitives stay hidden in the hayloft for three days. Nobody disturbs or frightens them. People bring horses in, feed them, take them out again, but nobody climbs the ladder to the loft. Perhaps the carriage driver has told his friends to ignore them. Perhaps they're simply lucky. Jane sneaks out to fetch food and to listen to the talk of the streets and the nearby market. She's a flower-girl. Nobody notices her. Except once, when she pauses on a street corner. She is not there for two minutes before another, slightly younger girl walks up to her, stands very close, and whispers fiercely in her ear. "Get your skinny arse out of 'ere now double quick. An' if I catch you 'ere again, you'll be in the river my girl, so help me God. And dead. Now **** off."

Jane doesn't find the streets of London so very different from the streets of Amritsar, or Bombay. The same complicated hierarchy of rights and obligations. The same interwoven relationships, opaque to any outsider. The same constant undercurrent of violence and fear. Fear of authority, fear of hunger, and fear of the Other, however it might show itself. Family is the most important thing here, because it's all most people have. So in some ways Jane doesn't feel out of place. She recognizes so much, and knows not to get involved. She moves away from the girl at the corner.

By the afternoon of the third day, Lak is recognizable again. He's not exactly what you'd call normal, but he's well enough to be angry at his own weakness and impatient to move on. The question is, how?

COLONELS AND GENERALS

The General has never doubted that he did the right thing in sending to the Colonel. But after Jane and Elizabeth leave him, he begins to see that not everybody shares his clear, black-and-white view of the situation.

"Unaccountably sad, my friend," he says when James asks how he is. "Unaccountably sad. Haven't felt like this since I lost my puppy."

James nods with great sympathy. He knows what it is to lose a puppy.

"Duty. We must all do our duty," the General continues. "You agree?"

*Of course." The merest hint of a hesitation.

"You think I was wrong."

"We must all do our duty as we see it …"

"You think I was wrong." The General leaps to his feet. "Must go to London. See what I can do." He strides out of the inn. James ups and follows like a faithful hound, always excited by an expedition.

And shortly after (only two days later), they sit with the Colonel in his secret office. Of course, the General has heard nothing of the escape. He has simply come to find out what has happened to Lak, and attempt to make peace with his sister and his niece. The news that they have disappeared together – and in such an admirable manner – throws him off balance, and rather delights him.

"And you've no idea where they are?"

"None at all, General. Though you can be certain they cannot go far. Every road and every ship out of the city is watched. We'll catch them, never fear."

The General can't stop himself smiling. Whatever the rights and wrongs, he can't help but marvel at these women. Dashed proud to have them in his family.

"Well, then. I'll trouble you no longer, Colonel."

"General … you'll let me know if you hear anything of your niece?"

"Of course, Colonel." But this time neither of them are sure how much he means it.

"Oh, splendid gel!" James is ready to celebrate, and the General has no objection to joining in. But his mood becomes more serious after the second cup of wine.

"How are we to find them, James?"

James thinks for a while – an activity that has not previously occupied a great deal of his life.

"What could we do if we did find them, General?" he says soberly. "Where can they go? It seems that our help can only mean five people in prison instead of three. Or worse."

The General feels that he is right. It makes him angry to be so helpless, and though he tries to cheer himself up with his usual medicine, this time the wine doesn't work.

PAY THE FERRYMAN

Indeed, there seems to be little hope for Jane and her companions. London is a big city, and with luck three people might succeed in hiding for a very long time. The difficulty comes when they want to leave.

"I don't see how we can be safe anywhere," Elizabeth says. "If we go to my brother, they will find us there. Anywhere we go they will find us and we shall be locked up."

"And most probably hanged," Lak says. The thought is a shock. Suddenly they see the real truth of their danger. A dull silence falls over them.

"So if we can't stay in this country, we must choose another," Elizabeth says.

"India," Jane says, but she isn't sure what she feels. "But how can we get to a ship? The Colonel will have men at the docks."

"I know how we might do it," says Lak. "But it will mean danger – most of all for you, Jane."

"It's hard to see how the danger can be any greater …"

Lak nods. "Good. Take this. Let's hope you don't need it." He gives her a knife he found in the stable. Someone has lost it – or thrown it aside because the blade is chipped. But it's sharp. Jane nods and puts it in the pocket of her dress.

Night in the streets. Puddles of people gather outside drinking establishments which span the entire range from unbelievably filthy to hellmouth. A few weak candles, a few dirty lanterns lift these groups from the surrounding darkness, but between them the streets are dark as pitch. And through these streets Jane is finding her way.

She is in search of a riverside inn at Rotherhithe, where a friend of Lak's will (they hope) be drinking. From there she will go to the dockland house where Lak took her when he kidnapped her. She is looking for the friend who stayed while the others travelled on the ship. She can't use a bridge to cross the river, because the Colonel's men are likely to be watching the bridges. So she is going some way downstream of all of them and hoping Lak's Rotherhithe friend will row her across.

It's only a couple of miles along the river from the stables, but it takes as many hours in the darkness – and when she eventually finds the place, she stands outside in the night for quite a few minutes more.

She plans to slide through the door unnoticed, in the hope that she can have a good look around for Lak's friend. But the room falls silent as soon as she appears. They're not used to strangers – and a visitor so late at night can only mean trouble.

Every eye in the room watches as she forces herself to keep walking towards the greasy waiter. Every head turns to follow her, automatons driven by a single impulse.

"Can I have some w...water, sir? I'm terrible thirsty."

Without a word, he plonks a mug down and fills it from a pitcher. The silence grows heavier; the sound of her swallowing the loudest in the room.

"Thank you, sir ... I'm looking for Jess Hexham ..."

There's a new intensity to the silence.

"I'm to say, the monsoon is late."

This causes a ripple of attention as if a very tiny stone had been dropped into the room. But still nobody says a word. Jane feels as if she is about to cry. She turns and begins the long journey across the room to the door. As she pulls it open, a hand falls on hers. She looks round. What she sees is not encouraging. A twelve-year-old (she guesses), ferret-featured boy; he leans forward to whisper in her ear. "Jess is my old man. Come out and say your piece."

They stand in the deepest shadow. She can hear the lapping of the Thames nearby and smell the sour smell of the river. "I need to cross the water," she says.

"It ain't free."

"I can pay."

"'ow much?"

"Now."

"'ow much?"

"How much do you want?"

"Two shilling."

"Very well."

"Each way."

"I only need to cross over."

"But I has to come back, don't I?"

"All right."

He grabs her wrist and pulls her towards the river.

"Them steps is slippery."

She has to feel her way down the steps on her hands and knees, so that — as she will see later — her skin and her clothes become stained with green river-slime. She hears the knocking of the boat's wood against the step and his hand grabs her arm again to guide her into the boat. When she is safely seated at last, she finds that her eyes have become more accustomed to the dark, and she can see the shape of the houses on the opposite side of the river and the shadow of the steps and the wall above her.

He begins to row, pulling upstream against the current so that the flow will take them back where they want to go. The river is wide, and the crossing takes a long time. Jane begins to worry that the sun will rise before they reach the other side. And then, somewhere out in the middle of the river, he stops rowing.

"What's the matter?" she says.

"I want me money now."

"Yes, of course." She pulls her purse

from her skirt and counts out two shillings, feeling the coins with her fingertips and pressing them into his palm.

Quick as a snake he strikes out and seizes the purse from her hand, pushing her with his other hand so that she falls on her back in the bottom of the boat.

"Thanks for the little extra," he laughs and turns the boat round again. She pulls herself upright again.

"Where are you going?" she cries.

"Shut it, or I'll chuck you over."

She can be quick as a snake, too. She knows this, because she played with snakes when she was smaller and befriended a so-called snake charmer, who taught her some of his tricks – not being concerned that a seven-year-old girl would be much competition to him.

She pulls the blade from her other pocket, lunges forward, and holds it against his throat.

"I will have my purse. You will take me across, and you shall have your four shillings. You understand?"

He laughs, not even pausing in his rowing. "Naa. You ain't gonna do nuffink wiv that."

She presses and pulls the knife slowly across his neck. The blood shows even against the dirt. He yelps and snarls, but she is careful to keep the knife against him. She has gone too far to back off now. If she relaxes for one second, he will throw her over the side. It's a long and uncomfortable voyage for both of them – but at last she can grab her purse from him and step ashore. The tide is still low enough for her to land on the beach. She hopes she'll find some stairs before the water rises again, but at least she can more quickly be rid of her troublesome ferryman.

"Your other two shillings ..." She throws the coins into the boat and stands with knife in hand on the beach until he is safely out on the water.

The sky is turning grey by the time she has climbed from the beach to the streets. She has no need of a disguise. Nobody gives a second glance to her filthy clothes and smudged face. She is very tired by the time she finds Lak's friend. Another step, and she feels she will collapse. They don't recognize her at first, and then treat her with great suspicion – especially when she talks to them in Punjabi. She tells them everything – how Lak was shipwrecked; how he found her mother again; how they came to be in hiding in Southwark. She trusts them because she has no choice. Slowly the atmosphere becomes more friendly. At last she has finished. She leans back against the wall and waits while they talk amongst themselves. It's a lively discussion, but she can't hear most of what they say. After a little while a boy appears and gives her a mug of chai, which she drinks, grateful for the warmth and sweetness.

At last the discussion comes to an end. One of the men leaves the room. There are three remaining, including Lak's friend, who now looks at her encouragingly. She doesn't know the other two.

"We will help if we can, but we must talk to the ship's captain. This will take some hours. You can sleep."

Just like a very tired toddler, she doesn't want to sleep at all, and she keeps her eyes open purely through strength of her pride. But once she's alone in the room, she finds her eyelids becoming steadily heavier. And then she is waking up and the afternoon has gone and night is falling again.

"He has agreed. You can sail for Bombay in three days. But you will have to hurry."

"Why 'hurry'? It doesn't take three days to get here."

"Lak cannot come here. There are always soldiers in the docks. You will travel down the river beyond Tilbury Fort to the place known as the Isle of Grain. This will take two days. You have little time to spare. The place is on the southern side of the river. Lak will not have to cross. There you will wait for the ship. You will signal and they will send a boat to collect you. And so they will take you to Bombay."

Jane jumped up and embraced him. "Thank you. Thank you …"

He took her arms and moved them gently away. "This will need money," he said.

"Yes, yes …"

He nodded. "Good. Then tonight we will take you back across the river." He lightly stroked her face. "Go well, my child."

VAGABONDS

It's after midnight by the time she is back in the hayloft. They debate whether to start out immediately or to wait. Whenever they leave, the first part of their journey must be at night. It's too great a risk to move through the streets of the city in daylight. Once they have reached the fields of Bermondsey and open countryside, then they can relax a little and travel by day.

"It's too late tonight," Elizabeth says. But Lak doesn't agree.

"We won't have another chance. If we are late, we will die. It's a long way. We should go now. Straight away. We'll be out of the city by dawn."

And so they leave their sanctuary, placing a few coins on the bare floor to thank the unknown person who left them undisturbed in their time of need.

Of course, they know that the Colonel's men cannot be on every road and every bridge and every coaching inn to catch them. But they have no way of knowing where the danger lies, and so they are compelled to behave as if it were everywhere. They walk in darkness through the grimy streets of the neglected south side of the Thames, until they pass at last from the city into the fields and country roads of Kent. But even then, they dare not take a coach; dare not even take the broad highway, but keep to the smaller roads where fewer people walk, and hide whenever they see anyone else.

It doesn't take long for the mud and dust of the road to stick to them, so that soon they look almost like figures moulded from the mud itself. More than once as they pass a farm, children throw sticks and stones at them, beggars on the road – and more than once the adults add their own kicks and curses. The journey cannot take more than two days, but often it feels much longer. The distance is forty miles for a crow, but nearly half as much again along the twisting hidden ways they choose to walk. Often they lose the way and waste time searching for somebody to ask. Many times there is nobody who knows, and all they can do is look for a road close to the river and follow it downstream toward the sea, hoping not to miss the piece of marsh where they are to meet their ship.

And then, on the morning of the third day, they cross a smaller stream as it flows towards the mighty Thames. They walk with difficulty across soggy marshland and then tussocky grass and sand and mud until they stand on the edge of the river – which is now three miles wide.

And they wait.

There are ships in plenty. And boats of all sizes. How can they know which is the one for them? They can only hope it sails close enough for them to read the name, since they are not sailors who can recognize a ship from its shape.

And how can they be sure that they're in the expected place? They believe they are, but there is so much river and so much shore.

It's cold and windy. They are tired, wet, cold. The watery sun has gone and the sky begins to darken. The day is nearly over. Nobody wants to be the first to speak, but they are all sure that the ship has gone. They are all miserably beginning to think of what they can possibly do next.

Jane sees it first, though it's hard to

be sure in the twilight.

"There ... the flag ..."

"Yes. Yes, it must be."

And again, Jane is first to begin jumping, waving her arms, shouting. Lak and Elizabeth quickly join in. *Please see us. Please be the right ship.* The plea thumps again and again in their heads like a wasp against a window. Surely only one ship would fly the flag of the Punjab – it being such a dangerous thing to do here, at the very heart of British power. And what other ship would lower its sails at this point in its journey?

The ship puts a boat down into the river. But Lak is not yet at ease.

"It might be a trap," he says. "Be ready to run."

But they don't have time to be cautious. Four men row the boat with great energy across the water to the shingle where they stand.

"Quickly," shouts one of them. "Or the ship will be gone ..."

For the ship, though it carries little sail, continues to travel at some speed with the tide and the current. There's no time to think. They fall into the boat which pulls swiftly in pursuit of the ship, where they see the Punjabi flag rapidly coming down again. They still don't know for sure whether they're with friends or whether these are the Colonel's men in disguise.

But this time – just for once, Jane thinks – everything turns out well. This is indeed the captain who will take them to Bombay – as long as they have the necessary funds to pay their passage. This is the ship that will be their home for the next few weeks.

Next morning, and the sun shines on Jane, her mother, and Lak. With a brisk following wind, the ship passes eagerly down the Channel and away from England.

Lak and Elizabeth stand side by side, arms around each other, and smile at Jane.

"A new beginning for us all," Elizabeth says. Her eyes shine with happiness.

"A new beginning," Jane echoes.

But she can't make herself quite as pleased as they are. She is really, truly happy to be going back to a life in India. But she knows it's going to be so much more complicated than it was before. She feels herself divided in so many ways. She still mourns her father, and though she has found a mother, she is also tied to the very person who was the cause of her mother's desertion in the first place. She doesn't know what she feels.

And, more than this; the General has shown her that she should be loyal to England, the country of her father and mother. And, to an extent, she is. But even more strongly she belongs to the places where she grew up, and the people of the Punjab. She knows that she is on her way to a fight in which she will have to take sides. Her mind tells her that she belongs to the British and she knows exactly what she ought to do; but her heart says she will fight beside Lak, and not for England.

Whatever happens, she knows it will not be easy. Whatever happens, she knows that she will stay true to what she thinks is right. And for now … she is looking forward to seeing Sandeep again. Just to show him that he was wrong when he said she was going away forever.

THE END

HISTORICAL NOTE

Sadly, all the main characters in the story are fictional (and all but three of the others). But the background is not.

The unruly Punjab in north-western India was a thorn in the side of the British right to the last days of the Empire. At the time of Jane/Suri's story, it was an independent Sikh Kingdom. The British invaded in 1839 and annexed it as part of British India – the Raj.

The real people? Dean Mahomet really was owner of the Hindoostani Coffee House, and the building still stands. It's even still a restaurant – now (at the time I write this) Japanese.

The Hangman William Brunskill was also a real person, as was his assistant, John Langley – who was indeed married with three children, though not much is known about either of them as people to spend time with.

The London coaching inns named and visited really existed, as did the

George and Pelican Inn in Newbury (more often known as the Pelican, and – according to Samuel Johnson, who once stayed there – aptly named, from the size of its bill). The Pelican Theatre was still standing in the 1970s, when it was finally demolished – though by then the building was used as a warehouse and hadn't been a theatre for a very long time.

The *Gothick* of the title (not a spelling mistake) refers to a tradition of romances popular in the late 1700s and early 1800s, which usually involved maidens in distress and ruined and/or gloomy castles in wild landscapes. Perhaps most famous of these are Horace Walpole's *Castle of Otranto* and Ann Radcliffe's *Mysteries of Udolpho*. But the initial inspiration for this book was Jane Austen, whose first full-length work, *Northanger Abbey*, makes fun of these gothick novels. Catherine, Austen's heroine, sees mysteries and dark plots everywhere, but none of them are real. I also acknowledge a debt to Thomas Love Peacock, whose comic gothick novels *Headlong Hall* and *Nightmare Abbey* are echoed in the name of the General's house.

About the Author

Ian Lewis is lucky enough to have travelled the world writing and directing documentary films for television. Additionally, he has written episodes of the children's animation series, *Mona the Vampire*, two feature films, which he also directed, five previous books: *How to Conquer the Internet, Get Down on the Internet, Kathmandu, Guerrilla TV*, and *Ghosthunter*, and many feature articles for print and online publications. He divides his time between rural Herefordshire in England and Vienna, Austria. Visit him on www.storymachine.co.uk.

CPSIA information can be obtained
at www.ICGtesting.com
Printed in the USA
LVHW031504241220
675096LV00002B/186